Yakim is a bodyguard to the prince of Hell's consort, and he likes his life as it is. He could do with fewer attempts by the mysterious society to unravel Berith's work and take over Hell's throne, but he's satisfied with his life. As a half-demon, half-human hybrid, he never expected to rise so high in the ranks of the demons serving Berith.

He certainly didn't expect to catch the eye of the king of Hell.

Lucifer is visiting Berith to meet his new human consort and to talk about the secret society plotting to take his throne. He'd be amused if it didn't happen at least once a year, but his family might be involved this time, and he dislikes dealing with them.

At his welcome ball, he can't look away from one of the consort's bodyguards, and while he realizes how complicated this would become if he attempted to seduce him, he can't get him out of his head.

Yakim has never aspired to be more than a bodyguard and wouldn't know where to start being the king of Hell's consort. The two of them are too different to make any kind of relationship work.

But even if they do manage to make it work, it might not be for long, because the society wants Lucifer's blood, and they won't stop until they spill it.

A Demon's Duty
Copyright © 2024 Catherine Lievens
ISBN: 978-1-4874-4100-5
Cover art by Angela Waters

Published by eXtasy Books Inc

Look for us online at:
www.eXtasybooks.com

A Demon's Duty
Demons Destinies 5

By

Catherine Lievens

CHAPTER ONE

"How long until we arrive?" Lucifer asked.

Bretton, one of his best friends and his personal assistant, looked down at his tablet. "We should almost be there." He wrinkled his nose. "Was it necessary to visit? I'm sure Berith could have done this on his own."

He *had* done it on his own. When he'd contacted Lucifer to tell him about the society, Lucifer hadn't been surprised to find out about it. Many people wanted power, and it made sense that some would organize into a society trying to get rid of the princes of Hell. It wasn't the first time it happened, and it wouldn't be the last. Sometimes they were successful and managed to kill the prince they targeted, and other times they failed miserably.

They had in this case. Berith had learned about the society and gotten rid of the members hiding in his palace. Then he'd let Lucifer know that from what he'd discovered, there were more members, some of them in Lucifer's palace.

Hence, Lucifer was here.

"He's a very capable prince," Lucifer agreed.

Bretton glared at him.

Most people didn't dare look at Lucifer that way. Most demons kept their distance and skirted around him when they couldn't. Bretton never had that problem. Even when they'd first met, he'd been respectful but had called Lucifer on his bullshit, which was one of the reasons Lucifer had wanted him to work for him. He needed people who would be honest with him instead of catering to his every need and telling him he was right every time he did something, even when it was obvious he wasn't. Only a few people could do that, and Bretton was one of them.

Lucifer relaxed in his seat. "Do you have a problem with Berith?"

Bretton sighed and put down his tablet. Lucifer didn't fully understand how the technology worked here in Hell. He just knew it did, and he was thankful for that. He needed to relax at the end of a long day, and there was nothing better than a TV series and a cup of tea to do that.

"I don't," Bretton said. "As you said, he's a very capable person. He hasn't been giving us any trouble, and he's followed orders. He has a strong hold over his subjects, and as far as I could find, they respect and even love him. Most of the people who live here don't want things to change."

"And you think my arrival will change things."

"I know it will. People aren't used to seeing you. You spend most of your time in your palace, and people don't know you. They only know about you, and you're aware of the kind of gossip flying around."

Lucifer grinned. "How many wives do I have by now?"

Bretton huffed, clearly not finding the situation as funny as Lucifer did. But Lucifer didn't exactly find it funny. He just took it that way because otherwise, he'd spend his days screaming.

"We're at five," Bretton said stiffly. "And there are rumors about you visiting Berith to take a sixth spouse. Some even say you're interested in his consort."

Lucifer snorted. "As if I'd take away anyone's consort." He never would, even if they weren't as in love as Berith and Mel.

"You might not want to steal them, but some of them wouldn't hesitate to throw themselves into your bed."

Bretton was right, and it had happened before. That was why Lucifer had several bodyguards and why Bretton spent a lot of time with him. That, and Lucifer didn't enjoy feeling lonely, which was incredibly easy even when people surrounded him. Lucifer knew all of that since he'd been in charge of Hell for many decades, but sometimes, it still surprised him.

The vehicle they were traveling in jerked sideways, and Lucifer leaned forward to peer outside. He could have traveled by portal, but he enjoyed seeing Hell as he traveled through it. Many people didn't. It was too hot and dusty, and when in the desert, it could be dangerous. Lucifer didn't care. He could defend himself easily from most demons and attacks, and traveling like this meant he could spend more time away from his palace than he would have if he traveled by portal. In his view, it was a win-win situation.

He was excited to see that the city he'd noticed in the distance a few hours ago was much closer now. From where they were, he could see a big palace at the center of it, and he knew that was where they were headed. It wouldn't be much longer at all, and he leaned back in his seat, grinning at Bretton. "Do you already have everything planned?"

"Of course. I talked to Sabin, and he sent me a schedule."

"I'm surprised the two of you have never been together. You share a passion for schedules."

"We like schedules because we're personal assistants to a king and a prince and need everything to be in order," Bretton said primly. "It doesn't mean it would work between us. How could it, when we live so far away?"

He wasn't wrong, and since Lucifer was only teasing, he let it go. He knew from Berith that Sabin had found love, so even if there had been a possibility of anything happening between him and Bretton, it was gone. Besides, Bretton had always been too focused on Lucifer and being the best personal assistant ever. The few times Lucifer had suggested he take some time off or slow down a bit so he could find someone and maybe build a family, he'd looked at him like he was nuts and had ignored his suggestions.

It only took them another twenty minutes to reach the palace. By the time they did, Lucifer was ready to get out and stretch his legs. He wasn't sure how long they'd been sitting, but it felt like years, and he didn't have infinite patience like Bretton.

As soon as he got out, a gaggle of servants rushed forward. It wasn't the first time Lucifer had visited, and he looked around, knowing who he needed to greet first. It would be one of two people, and he bounced on the balls of his feet as he waited.

A tall woman appeared. Her skin was pale green, her hair was long and white, and she wore a gown that told everyone her status at the palace. She glided instead of walking. When she reached Lucifer, she held out a hand with three long fingers in welcome. Lucifer took it and bowed his head.

"Your Highness," she said.

"Please. I already told you to call me Lucifer."

Meana pulled her hand back and curtsied. "Only if you call me Meana."

"I always do. Where's Olin?"

"Busy organizing the ball to celebrate your arrival."

Lucifer groaned. "It's no use telling the two of you I don't want a ball, is it?"

"You know better than that, your Highness."

Lucifer did. He had to go through these parties any time he traveled out of his palace. They were meant to welcome him and give people the opportunity to see him from afar and maybe even talk to him. Usually, they irritated him, but he didn't quite feel that way here. He liked Berith and was looking forward to an evening of relaxation before they had to get to the point of his visit and talk about the society.

"How long do I have to get some rest and clean up?"

"As long as you need, your Highness."

Meana and Olin were the two people in charge of everyday life here at the palace. They organized everything and kept the servants in line, and they were extremely good at their job. One of them always welcomed Lucifer when he visited, ensured he had everything he needed, and told him more about the schedule.

"We both know that's not true," he teased. "I'm sure you and Olin have organized everything down to the second. Email everything to Bretton, will you?"

"Of course, your Highness. A servant will show you to your rooms."

Lucifer nodded and followed the servant Meana had gestured to. The woman kept glancing at him, and he grinned, his smile widening when she jumped slightly.

Most demons feared him. He had a reputation and was one of Hell's strongest demons. He wasn't the king of Hell for nothing. Sometimes, he wished people would see him for who he was instead of what he was, but this visit wouldn't be that time.

He sighed. He was eager to see Berith and finally meet Berith's consort, which wouldn't happen if he wasted time. "Show me the way," he told the servant.

She rushed forward, and Lucifer followed.

Yakim didn't like parties and balls. They were noisy and crowded, and they made it harder to keep an eye on Mel. With so many demons around, it was imperative that the consort be protected, and doing so during a ball made Yakim and Roque's lives harder. Roque didn't seem to mind, but Yakim did.

"How long is this thing?" he muttered.

Roque grinned at him. "You really want to run back to your

room already?"

"I want Mel to be safe."

"He is. He has us, doesn't he?"

He did. Berith had assigned Yakim and Roque to his consort's protection soon after Mel arrived at the palace, and they'd kept him safe since then. Mel was a sweet human, and while he was aware of how harsh Hell could be, he led a protected and sheltered life at the palace. Berith wouldn't have it any other way, and Yakim understood why. Mel was precious, and he was changing things in Berith's territory in a way no one had expected, but everyone was grateful for it. Life was easier for everyone, and as far as Yakim was aware, most of the demons living in Berith's territory loved Mel. The demons who belonged to the society didn't, but they were outliers.

That didn't mean Mel didn't need protection, which was where Yakim and Roque stepped in. Usually, it was fairly easy to keep him safe. Mel led a quiet life. He might be consort to a prince of Hell, but he was happy being a teacher to the children who lived at the palace. He spent most of his days doing that, then he had family time with Berith and the rest of their people. He seldom left the palace, something for which Yakim was grateful. It would be hard to protect any consort of a prince of Hell, but a human made everything more complicated.

The ball was a good example of that. Mel probably didn't realize how many people were staring at him, but Yakim did. He kept an eye on everyone, which wasn't easy considering how many demons had crammed into the ballroom. He understood the curiosity to see Lucifer, even from afar, but this was ridiculous. The demon was in charge of Hell because his father had been before him. Yakim had never met him, but he doubted Lucifer was special in any way.

He had to admit he was curious anyway. He knew Berith

and Lucifer were close and somewhat friends, which he'd been surprised to find out. If Berith liked Lucifer, the king had to be a good person, which wasn't what Yakim had expected.

He eyed the demon in question. Yakim hadn't known what to expect, but it wasn't this.

Lucifer had spent time with Berith before the party. Yakim hadn't been there to listen to their conversation since he'd been with Mel, and when they'd joined the prince and the king, Mel and Lucifer only had the opportunity to say hello to each other before having to walk into the ballroom. Lucifer had been respectful. He'd treated Mel like he would have if Mel had been a demon, and Yakim was glad. Mel was a gentle soul, and he didn't deserve to be treated harshly just because of what he was, like some demons did.

Lucifer had been a surprise because of that, but also because of the way he'd dressed. Yakim had expected something extravagant, but the king of Hell wore black instead. The suit was human, cut to perfectly fit his body, and made him stand out.

With the heat in Hell, most demons wore flowy clothing. Even Mel, who was human, had taken to the style. Lucifer didn't seem to feel hot, though. He moved as if he was perfectly comfortable in his suit and tie, and Yakim couldn't look away.

Lucifer appeared human. No one would doubt that he wasn't as soon as they got close to him, because he exuded power, but from where Yakim was, it would have been easy to make a mistake. There were no external signs of Lucifer being a demon.

He had long black hair styled at the back of his head. It looked soft and slick and reflected the buttery light in the ballroom. His black eyes seemed to take in everything around him, always with a smile. Even now that he was sitting at the table for dinner, talking to Berith's brother, Tobal, Lucifer was smiling. Tobal looked uncomfortable, which Yakim could understand. It had to be unnerving to have the attention of the king of Hell.

"Stop worrying so much," Roque whispered. "Mel is safe. He's not going to jump up from his seat and run away. No one can reach the table unless they're invited, and even if they could, Lucifer is there, along with Berith. Do you think either of them would allow anything to happen to Mel?"

Yakim glared at his friend. "I can't help but notice that you haven't mentioned either of us. We're the ones supposed to protect Mel."

Roque chuckled and winked. "It was implied."

Yakim turned his attention back to Mel, only for his gaze to lock with Lucifer's. Yakim knew how he should behave. He should quickly look down and bow his head, silently telling Lucifer he respected and feared him. He wanted to do just that, but he couldn't seem to look away. Lucifer wasn't looking away either, and Yakim found himself trapped. He swallowed, telling himself it was ridiculous.

Lon arrived. He excused himself for being late and sat next to Tobal, and Lucifer glanced away from Yakim to say hello. Yakim's shoulders slumped, and he relaxed.

What the fuck had just happened? Why had Lucifer been staring?

"What was that?" Roque asked in a whisper.

"What?" Yakim answered, acting as if nothing weird happened.

"You know that rumor about Lucifer having five wives?"

Yakim frowned. "What about it?"

"You think he wants to make you his sixth consort?"

Yakim growled but kept his attention on the table. Thankfully, Roque had had his fun, and he dropped it.

They spent the rest of dinner watching the table and the room from behind Mel and Berith. Once the food had vanished from the tables, it was time for dancing. It unnerved Yakim because he couldn't stay with Mel as he moved on the dance floor, but he told himself to relax. Berith was with him and would keep his consort safe.

But he wasn't the first to offer to take Mel for a spin. Lucifer did, getting to his feet and holding out his hand to Mel with a bow. He said something about dancing with the most beautiful person in the room, and Mel's cheeks flushed. It was adorable, and Yakim had to resist the urge to grin. He was pretty sure Mel hadn't expected Lucifer to be so charming. Yakim certainly hadn't.

Mel didn't hesitate to take Lucifer's hand, and Yakim watched them as they moved to the dance floor. They weren't the only ones. Tobal dragged Lon there, even though Lon looked like he'd rather have all of his teeth pulled out. But he didn't argue with Tobal. He loved him too much not to give him what he wanted.

Hell wasn't a loving place. It was harsh and cruel, and it wasn't often that demons allowed themselves to love. It wouldn't do anyone any good if they were seen as weak, but things were changing. Berith had never hesitated to show Mel how important he was to him, and it had a ripple effect on the people who lived in the palace and the city. The demons weren't ashamed to show they cared about their spouses anymore. They weren't afraid to love, and it was good to see. It was one of the reasons Yakim liked Mel, and as he watched him move around the room in Lucifer's arms, he once again promised himself that he'd do whatever he had in order to keep Mel safe. He was precious and meant the world to too many people for Yakim to allow anyone to hurt him.

Lucifer should be focused on the human in his arms. It hadn't been hard initially, but then Lucifer glanced up, and his gaze crossed with the gaze of one of the bodyguards standing behind Mel and Berith. Since then, the demon had been the only thing Lucifer could focus on, and it wasn't like him to be distracted, especially in a place where he might not be safe.

He considered how he felt about all of this. He was here to discuss the society with Berith and visit with him since he was one of his closest friends. They didn't spend nearly enough time together or even catching up on the phone. They both had heavy responsibilities, and knowing that Berith was in charge of this part of Hell meant that Lucifer didn't have to worry about it. He trusted Berith with his people and his life.

That was why he felt safe. He knew that Berith's people feared him, but they loved Berith. He was such a good prince that more demons were moving into his territory than ever before. Most of them didn't want Hell to be a place of pain anymore. They wanted to live their lives without struggling to find food or worry about getting killed, and they could do so in Berith's territory.

A big part of that was due to the man in Lucifer's arms. He looked down, wondering how Berith had gotten his hands on the small human. Mel was beautiful, and from the way he and Berith looked at each other, it was clear they loved each other very much.

"I don't think I've ever heard how you and Berith met," Lucifer said as he twirled Mel around the room.

Mel wrinkled his nose. "I was kidnapped from the human realm. The demon who took me gifted me to Berith. He thought that by doing so, he'd eventually be able to kill him and take his place here at the palace."

Lucifer needed to keep in touch with his friends. How could he not have known about any of this? "And you fell in love?"

"It wasn't hard. Berith is an easy man to love."

Lucifer wasn't sure about that. Berith was a demon, and it

was never easy to love a demon. Mel didn't seem to care about what Berith was, thankfully. He just loved him, and that was that.

Lucifer looked around for the handsome bodyguard again.

He didn't think he'd ever been in love. He'd liked people and had relationships, but none of them had turned to love. He'd certainly never wanted to make any of them his consort, yet Berith hadn't hesitated, even though Mel was human.

Lucifer had a lot to learn from his friend.

"You're not what I expected," Mel declared.

Lucifer grinned at him. "Please tell me I'm much more handsome than you thought I would be."

Mel laughed. "You are. I expected you to look more like a demon."

Lucifer had known he would. When demons first met him, they were always surprised and almost never recognized him as the king of Hell. "I don't need to look like a demon to be one."

"Oh, that's not what I was implying. Berith has assured me you're the most powerful demon in Hell, and I believe him."

"But you didn't think I'd look human."

"There are so many different demons even in this ballroom, and so many variations. I love the diversity, but I can't deny seeing someone who looks like me for once feels good."

Lucifer nodded. He couldn't fully understand where Mel was coming from because he was a demon, and more importantly, he was the king of Hell. He did know how he felt when he visited the human realm, though. It was good to be anonymous and not to have people falling all over themselves to do whatever he wanted. He could vanish in the background in the human realm, even with his bodyguards following him around. He was just one of many humans there.

Even though he wasn't human.

He'd always looked this way, and that would never

change. Some demons believed it meant he was part human, but they quickly changed their mind once Lucifer showed them how powerful he was. He knew how it felt to look nothing like everyone surrounding you, so he squeezed Mel tighter.

"You feel the same?" Mel asked.

"I won't deny it is pleasant," Lucifer admitted. "But I'm not sure if it's because we both look human or because you're such a sweet person."

Mel's cheeks flushed again. He was adorable, and Lucifer wanted to tease him even more. He was pretty sure Berith wouldn't be happy if he did, so he pressed his lips together.

"Thank you," Mel murmured.

"Oh, it wasn't a compliment. It's the truth."

He'd been excited to meet Mel after everything Bretton had to say about him, and he hadn't been disappointed. Mel might be human, but he had the respect of every single demon at the palace. When they bowed to him, it was because of the kind of person he was, not because he was Berith's consort. They loved him more than Berith, even though Berith was a good prince. He was even better now that he had Mel.

And everyone knew it.

"Can I cut in?" Berith asked, appearing next to them.

Lucifer grinned. "I'm tempted to whisk Mel away to my palace."

Berith scowled, but it was playful. "You could try."

"I'm not going anywhere," Mel said with a chuckle. "I'd be happy to dance with you, Berith."

Lucifer let him go. He watched as they turned to each other, and Mel melted in Berith's arms. They looked at each other with so much love that it made a part of Lucifer that he hadn't realized existed ache.

Would he ever have this? He didn't have a consort, contrary to what gossip said. He'd never wished any of his relationships to go that way, mostly because they all wanted something from him. They weren't with him because they loved him but because of what he could give them. A few had tried to push things into consort territory, but Lucifer wasn't an idiot. He hadn't trusted anyone to sit by his side on his throne, and he still didn't.

But part of him yearned for what he could see between Berith and Mel. Mel wasn't with Berith because he was a prince of Hell. He was with him because he loved him, and that wasn't something Lucifer had ever experienced. He hadn't even realized it was something he might want.

He turned to go back to the table, not one bit surprised to see that the two bodyguards who'd framed Mel earlier were still there. They were watching Mel and Berith, but their stances were relaxed. They knew Mel was safe in Berith's arms.

Lucifer sat and watched the guard he'd stared at earlier. He wasn't sure what made it almost impossible for him to look away.

The demon was handsome, but that couldn't be it. Lucifer was around lots of handsome people every day, but no one had ever caught his attention so completely the way this bodyguard had.

He was taller than Lucifer, but that wasn't difficult in Hell. Lucifer looked human, and he was sized like one. He was tall for a human, but not for a demon, so most of the people around him towered over him. The guard wasn't any different, and the twisted horns that rose from his forehead made him appear even taller. He had long fingers tipped with claws, dark and patchy skin, and white eyes. His white hair was short and exposed his pointed ears. Like most demons, he was a mix of different species, and it made him incredibly interesting.

And that was all there was to it. It had to be.

Yakim could feel someone watching him and didn't have to check to know who it was. He didn't understand why the king of Hell seemed so interested in him, but it didn't matter. He didn't care who was watching him as long as they didn't stop him from doing his job.

Right now, there wasn't much for him to do. Berith was dancing with Mel, and no one would dare attempt to attack the prince's consort when the prince was there. They probably wouldn't dare attack Mel even when he wasn't with Berith. Most of the people living in Berith's territory loved Mel and would never hurt either.

But not all. Some demons felt like Mel didn't belong by Berith's side or in Hell. They didn't want him here and wished to take Berith down from his throne. That was one of the reasons they'd created the society. The society had been dispatched, but only from this palace. Yakim hadn't been surprised to find out they were still out there, and it made him uneasy.

His only role was to protect Mel and Berith, but he couldn't protect them from an entire group of people intent on hurting them. He was only one demon, and even with Roque, they sometimes were stretched thin. Their priority was Mel, followed by Berith and the rest of their family.

Right now, they were safe, but how long would that last? The society was gone from the palace, but it was still out there, plotting. They wanted what most demons wanted—power, control over others, and wealth. They were ready to do anything to get that, but they'd have to go through Yakim to get to Mel, and he wouldn't let anything happen to the sweet human.

Berith and Lucifer had yet to meet to talk about the society, but from what Yakim had seen, he doubted Lucifer would work against Berith. He wanted to know who was undermining his authority in his own palace, and hopefully, he'd dispatch them quickly. Doing so would keep Berith and Mel safe for now. Plenty of demons in Hell wanted to take them and other princes down, but it was something Yakim would worry about when it happened. At the moment, his focus needed to be on the society and protecting Mel.

It was hard to do that when he could feel Lucifer watching him. He kept his attention on Mel and Berith, watching them move around the dance floor, but it was as if Lucifer's eyes were burning a hole in Yakim's forehead. He didn't understand why the king of Hell was watching him, and he wasn't sure he wanted to find out.

He had to be respectful, but he'd be firm if Lucifer tried anything with him. He didn't want to land in the king of Hell's bed. He had a job to do, and being another notch in Lucifer's bedpost held no interest for Yakim.

But even so, he couldn't deny how fascinating and handsome Lucifer was. Everyone was watching him, yet he was watching Yakim. It didn't make sense because he could have anyone he wanted in his bed with just one snap of his fingers, but Yakim hadn't seen him take an interest in any other people in the ballroom. The king was focused on him, which could end badly.

Yakim swallowed. If things came to that, he'd talk to Berith. Berith was under Lucifer when it came to Hell hierarchy, but that didn't mean Lucifer wouldn't listen to him. Besides, Berith was Lucifer's friend, and he wouldn't be if Lucifer was a bad person. Berith trusted him, and Yakim trusted Berith.

Everything would be all right. Even if Lucifer was interested in Yakim, Yakim doubted he'd force anything. Yakim just had to let him down gently so he wouldn't make an enemy out of the king of Hell, and things would be just fine.

He had to believe that because he'd run away screaming if he didn't.

CHAPTER TWO

The ball had been delightful, but that was yesterday. To-day, Lucifer had to face the reason he was visiting Berith — the secret society that was trying to kill his allies and take his throne.

He wasn't looking forward to it. He wanted to spend time with his friend and have fun, something that didn't happen often enough. One would think that being the king of Hell, Lucifer could decide when he wanted to work and when he could relax, but that wasn't what happened. Bretton had Lucifer's schedule under control, and he'd hurt him if he as much as thought to deviate from it.

So here Lucifer was, on his way to Berith's office. It wasn't the first time he'd visited the palace, so he knew where it was. He didn't have a problem walking down the hallways without a guide with his two bodyguards trailing behind him.

He ignored them. He didn't despise them or anything like that, but he strongly disliked the fact that he needed them. He wasn't even sure he did. As the most powerful demon in Hell, he wouldn't be hurt if he were attacked, or at least, that was what he'd told Bretton when his friend had insisted that he needed bodyguards. Bretton had ignored him and hand-picked these two, and while Lucifer knew it gave his assistant peace of mind, it annoyed him.

He didn't need those two trailing him like puppies. He needed to be left alone to defend himself, which he was more than capable of doing.

He stopped and turned to them when he reached Berith's

office door. "You can wait out here."

One of them nodded and took a step back, but the other frowned. "Bretton was clear that we needed to check the rooms before you went in," she said.

Lucifer resisted the urge to groan. "What do you think is going to be hiding in this office? The only person here is Berith, and he's not going to hurt me."

She looked like she wanted to argue, so Lucifer arched a brow. Her pale, light blue skin flushed, and she stepped back and stood next to the other bodyguard.

Lucifer was free, or at least, he was free of them for a few hours.

He knocked on the door and waited for Berith to open. When Berith did, he rushed inside, afraid the bodyguards would change their minds and decide to follow him in. Berith looked amused and peeked in the hallway before closing the door.

"You remind me of Mel when I assigned Yakim and Roque to him," he said.

Lucifer perked up. "Yakim and Roque?"

"His bodyguards."

Who was who? Lucifer hadn't managed to get the name of the guard who had caught his attention, and he wanted to know. It was ridiculous and wouldn't lead to anything, but it was a distraction, and he always welcomed distractions. "The two men bracketing Mel last night?" he asked.

Berith nodded and gestured at Lucifer to sit in front of his desk. "They've been guarding me and my family for years, and I trust them with my life. They've actually saved it a few times, so I knew they would be the best option for Mel. He didn't like that, though."

Lucifer grinned. "I imagine he didn't. He's independent."

"He is." Berith went to sit in his chair with a sigh. "I love him for that, but he needs to understand that he's not in the human realm anymore. He lives in Hell, and he's my consort. People are going to try to hurt him just because of that, and I don't want anything to happen to him."

Lucifer had known Berith loved Mel yesterday when he'd watched them together. Berith's words confirmed it. "The two of you are well suited."

Berith snorted. "I'm sure most demons don't think we are. He's human, and integrating him has been more complicated than I thought."

"It looks like everyone at the palace likes him." Lucifer hadn't noticed anything that would worry him, but it wasn't like anyone would come to him to complain about Mel, so what did he know?

"I think they do. But some of them don't think he should be my consort even though they enjoy talking to him. They think he's too weak and doesn't understand Hell as a consort should. I can't say they're wrong. His place isn't in Hell, but there's no way I'm letting him go now unless he wants to."

"He's never returning to the human realm," Lucifer said. He didn't have to ask Mel to be sure of that. "I believe you're stuck with him."

"I wouldn't have it any other way. Is Bretton coming?"

"He hasn't said anything about that. He's probably busy with my schedule or something. He's a bit obsessed."

"He and Sabin are so much alike."

"That's what I said!" Lucifer exclaimed, leaning forward. "I even asked Bretton why he and Sabin had never been together. I'm aware that Sabin now has a partner, but they would have been a good fit before."

"I don't know about that. From what I'm seeing, partners are better together when they're not as similar as Bretton and Sabin are. I'm pretty sure they'd both schedule to kill each other if they ever were to be together."

Lucifer could imagine it. It made him smile, and he realized that both he and Berith were wasting time. They were delaying the inevitable, and while Lucifer wanted to continue doing so because he wasn't up to talking about the society, he couldn't stay here forever. Eventually, he'd have to return to his palace, away from one of his best friends.

He wasn't looking forward to it.

He leaned back in his chair and linked his fingers on top of his crossed knees. "Tell me about the society."

Berith did. He told Lucifer about his half-brother Tobal and what had happened to him. Lucifer was impressed. Most demons would have sacrificed Berith and taken his place on the throne, but not Tobal. Instead, he'd done what he could to save his brother and succeeded. Now, he and Berith were a tight unit, and no one would ever come between them.

Seeing the fond way in which Berith talked about his brother made Lucifer think about his sister. They weren't close, and they never would be. Sometimes he felt that was a pity, but other times he was glad. She could create trouble like no one else, even when she didn't mean to, and usually, she did mean to. She'd been eyeing Lucifer's throne since he'd sat on it the first time, and Lucifer wouldn't be surprised if, eventually, she made a run for it. She'd have to kill him to get there, which he thought was why she hadn't tried it.

Lucifer might not love being the king, but he wasn't planning to give up the throne. He wanted to protect the few people important to him, and being king of Hell was the best way to do that. He'd never be able to change Hell, but he didn't need to. He just needed to keep it under control.

The only way for him to do that was to rely on his princes and the other dignitaries to take care of their responsibilities. Berith had done a good job and had stopped the spreading of the society in his palace. The same couldn't be said for many of the other princes. If the society had infiltrated Lucifer's palace, there were many more of them than Lucifer had expected, and they were sneakier.

And all of them were gunning for him.

He didn't know how long he and Berith talked. Berith went through a lot of details that made Lucifer's head ache, but he focused anyway. By the time Berith was done, Lucifer was starving.

His stomach growled as Berith explained how Lon had gone through every document found in the home of the minister who'd been working with the society instead of serving Berith. Berith arched a brow and stopped talking, and Lucifer shrugged.

"I'm hungry."

"I can hear that. Why don't we go to lunch?"

Lucifer was on his feet quickly. "Let's go. Is your Mel going to be there?"

"If I didn't know you, I'd think you wanted to steal him from me."

"I would never think about it, even though he's adorable. But no, I'm not interested in him. He's nice, though, and I enjoyed talking to him."

"You also enjoy staring at one of his bodyguards."

Lucifer should have known he hadn't been discreet enough yesterday. "You saw that?"

"Anyone with eyes would have seen it. He's Yakim, by the way."

Lucifer had thought he'd have to work harder to get Yakim's name, but he was glad he didn't have to. He still had no idea what he'd do with the knowledge or with him himself, but for now, he didn't have to come up with a plan. Maybe he'd think of one when he saw Yakim, but it would be fine even if he didn't. He had to decide what he wanted before he could think about what came next.

Yakim was with Mel in the dining room, watching him eat lunch, when the dining room doors opened. He straightened his back and exchanged a glance with Roque, and both of them turned their attention to the newcomers.

Berith came in, and Yakim relaxed, only to tense again when Lucifer appeared behind him.

The king of Hell seemed delighted. He looked around with a wide smile that made him look almost like a child. There was wonder in his gaze, almost as if he couldn't quite believe he got to have lunch with the people sitting around the table.

Not many people did. Only Berith and his family ate their meals in this dining room. It was private, and no one who wasn't invited by Berith would be allowed in. Yakim and Roque were here because they were Mel's bodyguards, but that didn't make them family. They watched as Mel ate with his family, and everyone talked over each other. Mel had offered to get them a place at the table, but both of them had refused.

Yakim couldn't imagine sitting next to Berith and making small talk. It was too odd to think about seriously, and he suspected that if it were to happen, he'd have a hard time speaking. He didn't get tongue-tied when he was with Berith the way he had early on, but that didn't mean he didn't respect him or that he wasn't intimidated.

He'd been a bodyguard for Berith for a long time. Initially, he'd been terrified that someone would yell at him or hurt him if he did something wrong or looked at them when he shouldn't. Instead, Berith and his family behaved as if Roque and Yakim belonged with them. Mel especially had pulled them into the family, and while Yakim and Roque did their best to keep some distance, it was getting harder every day.

Yakim could feel that someone was staring at him. It made his skin prickle, but he kept his gaze forward and on Mel. He already knew who was staring, anyway. The king of Hell wasn't discreet, which meant it was a small miracle that no one had noticed anything last night.

Yakim's gaze paused on Berith for just a few seconds. His prince's expression told Yakim that maybe someone *had* noticed something.

He quickly looked away and told himself to focus. He hadn't done anything wrong yesterday. He'd done his job, had kept an eye on Mel until he'd retreated to the suite he shared with Berith, and had gone to bed. He wasn't the problem here. Lucifer was, and he was still fucking staring.

"Did you have a good morning?" Berith asked Mel after kissing the top of his head.

"I've had better."

He started explaining the painting disaster that had consumed his morning to Berith, but Yakim couldn't focus on his words. He'd been there to see it happen, so he already knew everything. The problem was that since he wasn't watching Mel, he found his attention wandering and settling on Lucifer.

The king of Hell had piled a lot of food on his plate and listened to Mel as he ate. Everything looked normal, but Yakim didn't miss the many times Lucifer glanced his way. The way he looked at Yakim told him he was interested, but that couldn't be possible. Who would be interested in him? Certainly not someone like the king of Hell.

He was probably curious about Yakim, nothing more. Yakim didn't look human, but everyone at the palace knew his father was human. It didn't matter that Yakim didn't look anything like him. He was only half-demon, and many people in Hell disliked that.

Yakim had never faced discrimination from Berith, but some people intentionally avoided him. They didn't want anything to do with him because of what he was, but it wasn't a great loss. Yakim didn't want anything to do with them, either.

He had more than enough people who cared about him not to want to add more to his life. He didn't need anyone else, especially not people who thought he wasn't good enough just because of who his father was.

Lucifer continued listening to Mel and staring at him for the rest of the meal. It was becoming a distraction, but he wasn't sure how to deal with it. Should he mention something to Lucifer? Or should he go to Berith? He had no doubt the prince would believe him, but what could he do about it? This was Lucifer they were talking about. Berith might be powerful, but Lucifer was even more powerful, and while he didn't seem like a bad ruler, Yakim couldn't help but wonder what he'd do if Berith brought it up. Would he hurt him? Maybe kill him? Yakim couldn't even think about that possibility. He didn't understand how powerful demons thought and didn't think he wanted to find out.

He wasn't powerful. He was nothing more than a bodyguard and liked things that way. He didn't need to catch the attention of the king of Hell of all people.

Thankfully, Mel had a class right after lunch, so he didn't linger once he was done eating. He kissed Berith on the cheek, waved goodbye at Lucifer, and left the dining room, Roque and Yakim trailing behind him.

They walked in silence for a moment. The hallways were still empty, a sure sign that most people in the palace were still at lunch. It was a relief because it meant that while Yakim needed to be vigilant, nothing would happen to Mel.

"Why was the king of Hell staring at you?" Mel asked suddenly.

Yakim couldn't speak, but maybe he didn't have to. Maybe if he stayed quiet, Mel would think he had no answer. That would be for the best because he actually didn't.

"You noticed that, too?" Roque asked.

Yakim glared sideways at him. "What are you doing? You

shouldn't go along with this."

"Why not? I saw him watching you. I'm pretty sure *you* saw him watching you, too."

Yakim threw his hands in the air. "So what? What does it matter that the king of Hell was watching me?"

"As long as you're okay with it, it doesn't matter," Mel quickly reassured him. "I just want you to know that you don't have to do anything you're unwilling to do. I don't care if he's the king of Hell. If he hurts you in any way, he'll pay for it."

That was one of the reasons Yakim liked Mel as much as he did. Not only was he a soft and gentle human, but he was also fearless and ready to kick ass if anyone hurt his friends. Yakim was humbled by the knowledge that Mel counted him as one of his friends.

"You won't have to kick his ass because there's nothing between us. He's not going to hurt me because he doesn't have a reason or a way to do so."

Mel didn't look convinced. "He's intense, but even more so when you're in the room. Are you sure there's nothing between the two of you? Because it doesn't matter if there is. I don't care who you're with."

Yakim tamped down on the wave of affection that rose in his chest. Even though they were friends, he couldn't do anything as stupid as hugging Berith's consort in the hallway.

That wasn't all they were. Yakim was Mel's bodyguard, and his job was to keep him safe. It wasn't to get too close to him or hug him.

But it felt good to have his support, and Yakim smiled. "There's nothing between Lucifer and me," he promised. "How could there be? He's the king of Hell, and I'm just a bodyguard."

Mel frowned. "You're not just a bodyguard. You're my friend."

"You know what I mean. I don't know why he's been staring at me, but it's probably because he's trying to make sense of what species I am or something."

Yakim couldn't believe there was more to it, so he decided not to. Lucifer was just curious about him, and that was that.

"All right. Are you ready to tell me what's happening here?" Berith asked while Lucifer was still watching the door through which Yakim had vanished.

Lucifer turned his attention to his friend. "I don't know what you're talking about."

Berith rolled his eyes. "Of course you don't. Are we going to ignore the fact that you stared at Yakim for most of the meal? Or that you've been staring at him since yesterday during the ball?"

Lucifer should have known better than to think he could get away with it. Berith was observant. Of course he'd noticed that Lucifer was particularly interested in one of his people.

Lucifer didn't want to lie to one of his best friends, but he also wasn't sure what to tell him. Yes, he enjoyed watching Yakim, but how could he explain it to Berith when he didn't know himself?

"You don't have to tell me," Berith added. "But if there's something between the two of you, I'd like to know. He's not just one of my subjects. He's also a friend, and I want to be there for him if he needs me."

"You mean you want to be there for him if I hurt him?"

"Pretty much. I know you'd never do so on purpose, but you're the king of Hell. That's already dangerous enough as it is, and that's without adding Yakim to the situation. Unless you're serious about him, I'd be careful if I were you."

Lucifer slumped back in his chair. "I'm not serious about him because we've never even talked. I saw him last night for the first time."

"And you've been staring at him since then."

The conversation was getting frustrating. "I find him appealing. There's nothing wrong with that, and I don't think you're surprised. He's an interesting mix of demon species."

"He's also half human."

Lucifer shrugged. "So? You know I don't care about that kind of thing. I spend enough time in the human realm not to."

Berith nodded as if satisfied with Lucifer's answer. "Many people don't like him because his father is human. I've tried to police that kind of behavior, but so far, I've been ignored."

Lucifer fake-gasped. "Say it isn't so. People aren't listening to you?"

Berith scowled. "It's not that. Most people have never listened to me, and I'm fine with that. I'm not even warning you to stay away from him because I know you wouldn't hurt him. I'm just making you aware of the fact that the situation is more complicated than you might have expected. Yakim was born in the human realm. He told me his mother brought him here when he was only a year old, and he's never met his father. He's also never made a secret of the fact that his father was human, and it's made his life complicated. Things are improving, especially since Mel moved into the palace, but he's my consort, and people respect him. The same can't be said for Yakim."

"You really do care about him." Lucifer wasn't surprised, but he *was* stunned at the passion in Berith's voice.

"Of course I do. Yakim and Roque have been protecting my family for years. They protected my daughter before Mel came into the picture, and I don't want anything to happen to either of them."

"You say that as if you expect something to happen because of me."

"Not because of you. Because of the life you live and who you are. It's not the same, and I want you to know that."

Lucifer rubbed his forehead. "I do know."

Berith was respectful and would never use Lucifer to gain anything, even though they'd been friends for a long time. He was a voice of reason, and Lucifer should listen to him.

He sighed. He really wasn't looking forward to doing so. Instead of giving in to his friend's demands, he wanted to continue staring at Yakim and imagining what the two of them could do if they were together.

That would probably never happen. Lucifer might be interested in Yakim, but there was no way to know if Yakim was interested in him. Beyond that, things were already complicated enough. Lucifer had to deal with the society and probably another bunch of people in line to kill him. He didn't have time for a relationship, especially one in which he'd have to introduce his partner to the rest of the court. He couldn't *not* be serious about Yakim because of how important Yakim was to Berith, but there would be many questions and even more confusion. Yakim might even get hurt, and that wasn't something Lucifer could allow to happen.

No matter how attractive Yakim was and how much Lucifer wanted to get to know him, he wouldn't. It was better to keep their lives separate.

Lucifer always did what was better for the people he represented and cared about, and Yakim was one of those people.

CHAPTER THREE

Lucifer had enough of meetings. Berith had told him everything he knew about the society, so what more was there to say about them?

The problem was that if Lucifer was done getting information, he didn't have a reason to stick around, and there was nothing he wanted more than to do just that. He didn't want to go back to his palace, where half of the people wanted him dead, and the other half wanted to sleep with him.

He hated it. Berith's palace was far from peaceful, but it was so much more so than what Lucifer was used to.

He didn't mind being king. He wanted to do the best for the people who lived in Hell, and he'd done so since he'd first sat on the throne. What he disliked were the people who lived at the palace. Everyone wanted something from him and tried to find a way to obtain it. He'd been threatened, seduced, and more, and it never stopped. When he was home, there was always someone who needed something from him.

The same could be said while he was here, but it was different. The people around him were loyal to Berith, and they didn't bother Lucifer as much. They stared, but that wasn't enough to affect Lucifer.

Eventually he'd have to go home. In the meantime, he'd be on as many of these meetings as Berith felt was necessary.

This time, he wasn't alone. Bretton had insisted on coming, possibly because he wanted to make sure Lucifer wasn't wasting time. Lucifer might be the king of Hell, but Bretton was the boss of him, and Lucifer wasn't afraid to admit it.

Bretton had his tablet ready and had been taking notes

since they'd entered Berith's office. His fingers flew on the screen so fast that Lucifer had to look away because it made his eyes cross.

At least Yakim wasn't here to distract Lucifer. That would have made things much more difficult.

"I still have a hard time believing that some of your ministers were involved," Bretton said.

"I don't," Berith responded. "Usually, this kind of thing happens because someone wants my throne. I'm sure Lucifer has gone through it, too. They believe they'll be able to take control, which doesn't happen if they haven't already had a taste of it. They have power and wealth, and they want more. The society members won't be people living a normal life outside this palace. They will always be people who are already privileged and want more of everything."

Lucifer had never thought of it like that, but Berith was right. When someone had tried to kill him, it had seldom been a demon with nothing to their name. That happened sometimes, too, but not often — definitely not as often as someone from Lucifer's inner circle trying to kill him.

That was why he didn't have a lot of friends, and none but Bretton at the palace. It wasn't easy to trust people when they tried to kill you as soon as you turned around.

But right now, Lucifer was surrounded by people he trusted. Bretton was there, along with Berith. Berith's head of security, Lon, was present as well, as was Tobal, Berith's brother and Lon's partner. Lucifer didn't know him well, but if Berith trusted him, so did Lucifer. Berith wouldn't take in anyone who would be a danger to Mel, and he hadn't hesitated to welcome Tobal into his family. That was good enough for Lucifer.

Bretton frowned as he mulled over what Berith had said. "Since we're thinking that the members of the society are high up in the hierarchy, I have a few names I suspect might be involved."

He looked at Lucifer. He was hesitant now, as if he feared Lucifer wouldn't take it well. Lucifer leaned back in his chair. "My sister and father."

Bretton nodded. "I've been keeping an eye on them, and I don't have proof, but it's certainly worth looking into."

"Do what you have to do. I trust you with my life and know you'll never steer me wrong."

Bretton seemed pleased. He'd started as Lucifer's personal assistant, but that wasn't all he was anymore. They'd been working closely for so many years that they'd become friends, and most days, he was the only person Lucifer could be himself with.

"I'll have my spies look into what they've been doing recently," Bretton said with a nod before turning his attention back to his tablet.

"The society will be weaker since they've lost so many people," Berith pointed out. "But that doesn't mean they're gone. We need to be careful."

"Does that mean Lucifer will stay here for a while?" Tobal asked.

Everyone turned to him. He looked like he wanted to run, but Lon pressed a hand to his shoulder, and Tobal visibly relaxed.

"Why do you say that?" Lon asked.

"Well, we know the society is gone from this palace, but not from Lucifer's. We don't even know who's involved there, which means it could be anyone and that it's dangerous for him to be there. On the other hand, this palace is safe."

Lucifer grinned. He'd been trying to find an excuse to stay longer, but Bretton wasn't an idiot. He knew what Lucifer was doing, and he'd been warning him that they'd have to go back soon. Tobal had given Lucifer an excuse not to.

"I really should stay until we're sure I'm safe," he declared.

Bretton huffed. "No one believes you're doing this for your safety, so you can drop the act. You just don't want to go back."

"I don't like anyone but you there, and you're here with me."

"I didn't think the king of Hell would be so goofy," Tobal whispered.

It looked like he'd spoken before he could think about it, and he quickly snapped his mouth shut, but everyone had heard him.

Lucifer laughed. "I don't know why people think I'm serious. I might be the king of Hell, but I'm also a person. There are things I like and dislike, and I dislike my palace and the people who lived there quite a lot."

Tobal looked relieved that Lucifer wasn't going to burn him to the ground. "Maybe you should make some changes, then?"

Maybe he should. But that wasn't going to happen until he found who was in the society and got rid of them. He wouldn't be surprised if his family was involved, and he trusted Bretton to find out if they were. He wouldn't hide anything from Lucifer, which was one of the reasons he was such a good personal assistant. That, and he didn't take any of Lucifer's bullshit.

"I don't think there's anything else we can do until Bretton looks into the people he suspects are involved," Berith said. "And, of course, you're both welcome to stay for as long as you want."

Bretton groaned. "Don't say that. He's going to try to move into your guest room."

Bretton knew Lucifer too well. "Not a guest room," he argued. "I require a bit more space than that. The suite of rooms I'm currently staying in will do pretty well, though. I hope you weren't planning to use them for anything else."

Berith chuckled. "As I said, you're welcome to stay as long as you want."

Lucifer might have made this place his palace if it didn't belong to Berith already. There was nothing Lucifer could do to change that, but maybe he could find another palace.

The problem was that the vipers would follow him everywhere. There were too many of them embedded in the midst of the people and servants he needed every day, and he wasn't sure how to get rid of them or even if he could.

But he was going to try. He wanted what Berith had and not only the love he shared with Mel. He wanted a safe place to be himself, where people wouldn't be plotting to kill him. He wasn't sure he could ever have that, but he could certainly try.

"That's amazing," Mel told the tiny child beside him.

He was holding a piece of paper, and from what Yakim had gathered, the child had painted something for him. From where he was, Yakim could only see splashes of bright color. It didn't look like it was any good, but there was a reason Mel was a teacher and he wasn't.

He would never have the patience to deal with all these little children every day. He barely had the patience to deal with Roque, and Roque was an adult. He could be reasoned with.

From what Yakim had seen, that didn't work well with children.

But Mel knew what he was doing and seemed perfectly at ease in the classroom. Yakim had seen him turn a tantrum into a peaceful moment, and he still didn't know how the consort had done that. It didn't matter, but he wouldn't mind being able to calm down crowds like Mel did routinely. It would be handy in his job.

Maybe it was Mel himself. Yakim eyed him, wondering if

he was magical. He was entirely human, so it wasn't possible, but he *felt* magical.

Yakim couldn't help but wonder what his life would have been like if he'd met someone like Mel when he was as young as the children surrounding him. His life growing up hadn't been the worst, but it also hadn't been great. He'd been pointed at and teased because his father was human, something everyone seemed to know even though Yakim didn't look human. He didn't even know his father, yet everyone had used him against Yakim.

What would it have been like to have a father like Mel? Yakim didn't know anything about his father, so he had no idea if the man had tried to oppose his mother when she took him back to Hell. Had they talked about it? Had they fought? Had he tried to keep her and Yakim there with him, or had he been happy to see them go? Had he even known that Yakim existed?

Yakim doubted he'd ever find out. He didn't speak to his mother anymore and wasn't planning on going back. She hadn't been abusive, but she'd also never been a loving parent, and there was nothing there for Yakim to return to. He could demand answers about his father, but he didn't think his mother would give them to him. She'd decided long ago that Yakim's father didn't matter, and she'd only broken her resolution not to talk about him once, giving Yakim his father's name and the city he used to live in. After that, it didn't matter how many times Yakim asked, because she never would say anything more.

But that was fine. He didn't need answers. He didn't need to know what had happened when his mother decided to return to Hell. Sometimes it felt like a piece of him was missing without that knowledge, but he had a much better life than many demons who lived in Hell and the human world.

He had a good job, worked for a prince who didn't use

cruelty and fear to rule, and loved people he considered family. He was close to Roque, but not just him. He had many friends in the palace, including Berith and Mel, although even admitting that solely to himself was awkward. They weren't just people. They were the prince and his consort, yet Yakim knew that if he needed anything, they wouldn't hesitate to step in and help him. That made them family to him, and it was more than anything his mother had ever given him.

Roque knocked their shoulders together. "What do you think that looks like?" he whispered.

Yakim looked up to see that Mel had hung the painting the child had given him on the wall by his desk. Even now that Yakim could see it better, it didn't look like anything. It was just colors, and while it was pretty if he squinted, he didn't know how to answer Roque's question. "A rainbow, maybe?"

Yakim had heard about rainbows during Mel's classes. They didn't exist in Hell, but they seemed like they would be beautiful to see. The many colors of the painting reminded him of one, so maybe that was what the child had been trying to convey.

Roque cocked his head as he continued staring. "Maybe. I thought the purple thing at the bottom looked a bit like a cow."

Yakim snorted. "You don't even know what a cow looks like. You've never seen one."

"Neither have you. The cow in that book Mel read the other day was purple, though."

Yakim bit his lower lip so he wouldn't smile. The cow in the book *had* been purple. He'd noticed Roque's eagerness to know how the book would end. He and Yakim had never had what Mel was giving these children. They'd been raised in Hell when it was harsher than it was now. Life was still just as hard in some sections of Hell, but Berith had created a safe haven for demons who wanted a more peaceful existence.

They'd been flocking to his territory, and while it made some things complicated, it was also good to see that so many demons didn't want to continue fighting and killing each other.

These kids would have many more opportunities than Yakim could have imagined. They would feel love and happiness, and no one would tell them that they shouldn't. Maybe that was why so many demons felt drawn to Mel. Even though most weren't kids anymore, he made them feel cherished in a way they'd never been before. He could show them there was so much more to life than the violence they were used to.

That was one of the reasons Yakim would kill for him. He'd even die for Mel, because without him, Hell would become a darker place again, and he didn't want that to happen.

No one did.

Did Lucifer *need* to be king of Hell? He'd asked himself that question many times over the decades since he'd first sat on the throne, and so far, the answer had always been yes. There was no one else to do the job, at least not the way it should be done. Lately, though, he'd started thinking that maybe he didn't need to be the one in charge.

"You have that expression," Berith said.

Lucifer blinked at him. He tightened his hand around his cup of tea, knowing that Berith was probably able to read what he was thinking on his face. He was one of Lucifer's best friends, and there would be no hiding from him, no matter how hard Lucifer tried.

"You can't read my mind," Lucifer declared.

Berith arched a brow. "I think I can."

"What am I thinking about, then?" Lucifer quickly tried to think about something inconsequential, but his thoughts were all focused on the throne and Yakim. He didn't want Berith to know he was thinking about either of those things, so instead, he concentrated on his cup of tea and how he would need to go to the human realm soon to buy more of the precious beverage.

Berith sighed. "You can't step down."

Lucifer groaned. "How do you do that?"

"I might not be able to read your mind, but I know you well. It's not the first time you've thought about what your life could be if you weren't the king of Hell, and I can't say I blame you. Considering everything, I don't think I'd want to be in your place, either."

"But you make it look easy."

"Maybe it's because I'm not the king of Hell but only one of its princes. I do my best, and it's never easy, but it's not as hard as what you have to deal with every day."

"Maybe I shouldn't have to deal with all of that every day."

Lucifer could tell he sounded like a child, but he didn't care. Berith was one of the few people he could be himself with, and he had every intention of indulging. When he went back to his palace—*if* he went back—he wouldn't be able to do this anymore. Bretton would slap him upside the head for thinking that he shouldn't be king anymore, so Lucifer would never dare mention anything to him, but Berith was safe.

"You definitely shouldn't have to," Berith confirmed as he leaned forward. "But you keep Hell under control and allow the demons who want a family and a peaceful life to have them. This place would truly become the Hell humans think we live in if you weren't on the throne. Could you imagine your father or your sister guiding Hell?"

Unfortunately, Lucifer could. His father had been in charge of Hell before him, and it had been a disaster. There was a reason humans thought that the bad people who died went to Hell. It had been a horrible place, and in some ways, it still was.

It was hot and dusty, and living here was harsh. It wasn't always easy to find food, and a lot of demons had been abused and traumatized by their parents and the way they were raised. In turn, they made their own children's lives hard, and it repeated itself again and again.

Lucifer had tried to change that. Berith had, too, and it felt like together, they were having success. They wouldn't solve every single problem, and Lucifer doubted that Hell would ever become peaceful, but it had gotten better, and he didn't want that to change. He'd had to force his father off the throne and work hard for these results, and he wouldn't allow anyone to ruin it.

But that meant he needed to be the king. There was no way out for him, no matter how much he yearned for one.

"It's not fair," he whined.

"It isn't," Berith agreed. "And maybe someday you'll be able to allow someone else to take your place. For now, though, you don't have an heir. There's no one who could take your place and continue your work, so you're not allowed to step down."

If he tried, no one would stop him. Berith would be disappointed, but Lucifer was sure he could handle that. What he couldn't handle was Hell going back to what it had been when his father was in charge. He'd worked hard to change things, and even after decades, there was still so much work to do. Lucifer was tired, but it didn't matter. Life wasn't fair for him or most demons in Hell. They had to deal with what it had handed them, and they were all doing their best, including him. His life's work would be to make Hell a better place, and he had every intention of doing so. That meant keeping power until he found someone he trusted to take his place. He was tired, but he would continue fighting, and hopefully, he'd survive whatever the society was planning.

He had to.

CHAPTER FOUR

Lucifer could feel Bretton staring at him over breakfast. He did his best to ignore him, even though it felt like his gaze was burning a hole in Lucifer's forehead. He knew what Bretton wanted and wasn't willing to give it to him for a while. Saying so out loud would push Bretton to fight for it, and Lucifer didn't want that to happen. He tried to never use his authority and power over people he considered his friends, and he'd have to do that or bend to Bretton's will if they broached the subject they were both dancing around.

Lucifer going back to his palace.

Lucifer poked at a piece of egg. He was hungry, but thinking about going back was enough to make him stop eating. Was it so bad that he wanted some time for himself? That he wished to be around people who cared about him instead of people who cared about power and wealth? He didn't really mind being the king of Hell. He liked trying to make people's lives easier and had the power to do so, but he loathed the people trying to con him into giving them what they wanted.

The only person Lucifer trusted in his palace was Bretton. He could do without everyone else, especially the demons who threw themselves at him or tried to manipulate him. It took a certain kind of personality and guts to try to manipulate the king of Hell, and he was impressed sometimes, but all of it made him feel lonely.

"I heard you were changing your ministers," Berith said before taking a sip of coffee.

Lucifer put down his fork, grabbed his cup of tea, and

leaned back in his chair. "It's necessary. Some of them were chosen by my father when he was still in charge, and they're a mess. They work for themselves instead of trying to do what's best for Hell, and I don't condone that."

"How are you choosing who to put in charge?" Mel asked. "I mean, from what I understand, you don't trust anyone there. How can you put someone you don't trust in such a role?"

There was no easy answer. "The only person I trust with my life there is Bretton. If I thought I could tempt Berith away from this palace, I'd ask him to come and work with me. I know that's impossible, so I go with the people I believe are not as bad as the others."

"That doesn't seem great."

Mel sounded worried. Lucifer suspected it was because he knew Berith needed to find a few new ministers after discovering that at least one of his had been an active participant in the society trying to take him down. Mel couldn't help him much to make this kind of decision, but he was still anxious about it. It was sweet, and it made Lucifer yearn for that kind of relationship.

What would it be like to trust someone like Berith trusted Mel? Lucifer's relationship with Bretton wasn't like that. It was similar to Berith's relationship with Sabin or Lon and wouldn't change. Lucifer loved Bretton like a brother and was happy to have him by his side, but they could never be more than friends and coworkers.

Lucifer wanted more.

His gaze drifted to Yakim, who was standing behind Berith and Mel. His focus was on the prince and the consort, so he didn't notice Lucifer staring at him.

Again.

Lucifer had made it a habit, and he suspected that Yakim wasn't happy about it. Lucifer had done his best not to be obvious and even to stop staring, but it wasn't always possible. How could he not watch Yakim when he was standing there, looking strong and like he'd be a worthy consort to the king of Hell?

Whoever ended up in that role—if anyone ever did— would need to be strong. By becoming Lucifer's consort, they would put a target on themselves, and they'd have to be able to deal with that. They wouldn't have any official power, because that was all in Lucifer's hands, but whoever Lucifer chose as his consort would have his ear. Even though they wouldn't have an official position, Lucifer would still talk to them and ask for their opinion and advice. They could change things in Hell by using Lucifer, and everyone knew that.

That meant that the demons hoping to become Lucifer's consort would be angry and maybe try to take out the person he chose. His ministers would try to manipulate that person, and if they couldn't, maybe they'd try to kill them, too.

Lucifer sighed. He couldn't ask anyone to take on that kind of life. It wouldn't be fair. Maybe that was why he'd never found love. Even though he wished for it, deep inside, he didn't want anyone to be in danger because of him.

"We'll get to work choosing the new ministers as soon as we're back at the palace," Bretton said as he stared at Lucifer.

His silent message was clear, but once again, Lucifer ignored it. He didn't want to make Bretton unhappy, but he wanted to make *himself* unhappy even less. He knew that if he asked Bretton to stay for a bit longer, his friend would agree, but he wasn't wrong. They had a lot of work to do, some of which would need to be done at the palace. They had to talk to people, and it would be better to do so face to face.

Lucifer supposed he could open a portal and return for a few hours as needed, but he didn't want to deal with any of it. Berith had told him that he could stay for as long as he wanted, and he'd been tempted to ask if he could just move in. They'd joked about it, but he was more than ever convinced that permanently leaving the palace might be the best thing to do, and not only for himself.

It wasn't good for Hell and its demons if he dreaded going to work as much as he did. Lucifer would return because there was no alternative, but maybe there could be one.

What if he found another palace? He and Bretton could choose the people who would move with them, from the servants to the bodyguards, to everyone else. They could make sure no one working against them moved with them, including members of the society.

Of course, to do that, they had to find out who was part of the society. Bretton was working on it and knew the palace's inhabitants better than anyone, including Lucifer. Lucifer trusted him to find out who wanted his throne, and maybe once they did, Lucifer would be allowed to move.

But if he wanted to do that, he'd have to convince Bretton and find a place to live.

His gaze drifted to Yakim again. Maybe if Lucifer moved closer, they could finally explore what was between them. They hadn't talked about it, but Lucifer didn't think he was the only one yearning for more than staring. He would never take Yakim away from his home and his friends, and maybe he wouldn't have to.

Yakim wouldn't be the main reason Lucifer moved closer to Berith. He couldn't be, because they barely knew each other, even though Lucifer could feel deep in his bones that if they gave each other a chance, they could find what Berith and Mel shared. They could have a love so deep that it would make them the happiest they'd ever been.

Lucifer had his priorities. He needed to talk to Yakim, find out if there could be anything between them beyond flirting, and go from there. He wanted to move even if Yakim told him there could never be anything between them, but he prayed that wouldn't happen. Still, being away from the palace that had been his father's and was full of spies and vipers could only be good for Lucifer, and he was looking forward to making it permanent.

He was the king of Hell. If he wanted something, he got it.

Yakim didn't have to look in Lucifer's direction to know the king was watching him. He always was when they were in the same room, although Yakim found that he was being slightly more discreet now. Yakim didn't know if it was because he didn't want the people around the table to notice, but it was too late.

Everyone knew Lucifer watched Yakim. Roque teased Yakim regularly, while Mel seemed worried about it, which Yakim didn't understand. From what Mel had said, it was clear he wanted Yakim and Lucifer to be happy, and if it was together, it would be great, but there was some hesitancy he hadn't explained.

Yakim could understand why he felt that way. Mel was consort to a prince of Hell, and if anything were to happen between Yakim and Lucifer, he might find himself in the role of the king's consort.

He almost snorted. He was just a bodyguard. He'd never be the king's consort and didn't aspire to be. The thought was enough to make him break into hives and make his stomach churn. That kind of power and responsibility wasn't for him.

So he'd continue ignoring Lucifer. He couldn't confront the king of Hell about watching him without making it awkward, so it was better that way. If Lucifer tried talking to him, he'd turn him down as nicely as possible. He didn't think Lucifer was used to anyone turning him down, but Yakim had no intention of giving in to the attraction he felt for him.

Lucifer was a handsome demon, but that wouldn't be

enough. It didn't even matter that Lucifer was so much nicer than Yakim had expected. There couldn't be anything more between them.

It was hard to resist. Yakim couldn't help but wonder if the only reason he'd resisted so far was that Lucifer had kept his distance even as he watched him. The problem was that Yakim had been watching Lucifer, too. He'd seen how happy the king was to spend time with Berith and how true their friendship was. He'd seen how sweet Lucifer was with Mel, even when Mel asked questions no one else would dare ask the king of Hell. Lucifer never hesitated to answer if he could, and it was clear he respected Mel, even though he was human.

Lucifer didn't seem to care about that. He hadn't asked for Yakim to be replaced even though he was half human and appeared to like Mel. It would be hard not to. That meant that Lucifer was nothing like Yakim had expected and was hard to resist.

Just Yakim's luck.

Mel got to his feet. "I have to go. Class is going to start soon, and I don't want the children to be left alone."

"Would you mind if I came with you?" Lucifer asked.

He'd been sipping on his tea but quickly put down the cup. Yakim had found it weird the first time he'd seen Lucifer drink tea. He'd expected him to drink strong black coffee. There was a soft side to Lucifer that Yakim wanted to explore.

He couldn't.

Mel appeared delighted by the suggestion. "Of course not. Do you want to see the children?"

"I don't know about that. I'm not good with children and wouldn't want to scare them."

"I'm sure you're good with them. How often do you interact with children?"

"Not often. People don't usually bring their children when they visit me."

Yakim wasn't surprised to learn that, but he *was* surprised to see that Lucifer appeared disappointed. As far as Yakim knew, he didn't have any kids himself. He certainly didn't have an heir. That would be a problem if the society succeeded in killing him, but Yakim didn't want to consider it. He didn't know the king well, but he was sure that if Lucifer were to die, life in Hell would be much worse for everyone except the people who had killed him.

He and Roque followed Mel and Lucifer out of the dining room after they said goodbye to everyone at the table. They kept a respectful distance from the two, and Yakim tried not to listen to their conversation. It was none of his business, even though Lucifer kept peeking back as if to check that Yakim was still there.

Where would he be? He was Mel's bodyguard, and he took his job seriously. Where Mel went, so did he.

"Maybe I could prepare them," Mel said. "If they know you're coming, they won't be surprised."

"As long as you're sure I won't scare them."

"I think it would be a good opportunity for them to meet you. If you don't feel up for it, you don't have to, but it would be great."

Lucifer was always sweet and gentle when he was with Mel. Most people were, but Lucifer seemed especially so. Maybe it was because of who he was. He wielded a power no one else in Hell had, not only because he was the king. He was the most powerful demon and could kill with barely a thought, yet here he was, worried that he'd scare children. Yakim was still trying to make sense of the king, and so far, he hadn't been able to.

"I'll be happy to visit your children," Lucifer confirmed.

Yakim didn't have to see Mel to know he was beaming, because he bounced a little as he walked. If Yakim was honest, he was kind of excited, too. He was curious to see how the children would react to Lucifer, and even more so, how Lucifer would react to the children.

Lucifer and Mel talked about Lucifer's visit until they reached the area of the palace where the classroom was. Lucifer bowed lightly and took Mel's hand, raising it to his mouth to kiss the back of it.

"As always, it was a pleasure to talk to you."

"For me, too." Mel hesitated. "And thank you for indulging me in this. I realize you have work to do and that this won't help you in any way, but I want the children to see that their king is a good person."

"I'm not sure I am, but you make me feel like I can change for the better if I want. There couldn't be a better teacher for young children."

Mel blushed, and while Yakim was tempted to roll his eyes, he suspected that Lucifer wasn't saying all of that to charm Mel. He truly believed it, and Yakim couldn't say he disagreed. Mel was a wonderful teacher, and the children in his class loved him.

Lucifer hesitated as he stepped away from Mel. He glanced at Yakim, and since Yakim was already looking at him, their gazes locked. Yakim couldn't look away, and he didn't try. Instead, when Lucifer lightly bowed, he mirrored the gesture. His heart raced, and for a second, he wondered if Lucifer would try to kiss his hand as he had Mel's. It was ridiculous, but everything in their situation was.

Lucifer didn't try to kiss Yakim's hand. He quickly straightened his back, then turned and walked away. Yakim watched him go.

"I'm pretty sure he wants in your pants," Roque said.

Yakim shook his head. He had to stop thinking about Lucifer. "Well, he won't get in."

"I don't know. If I had the opportunity to sleep with the king of Hell, I don't think I'd say no. He *is* kind of terrifying, though."

"He's not," Yakim snapped. "He's nice and gentle."

Roque looked at him like he was nuts. "Gentle? He's the king of Hell."

But when Yakim glanced at Mel, he could see Mel understood what he was saying and agreed. Mel nodded and smiled at him, then gestured toward the door. "Shall we go in?"

Yakim was ready for the questions to end, so he quickly nodded.

No matter how nice and gentle Lucifer was, there would be nothing between them.

CHAPTER FIVE

Lucifer was convinced that his place was here, more than ever. Maybe not here as in Berith's palace, even though Lucifer loved it, but here in a place where people liked him and wanted the best for him. Here, where his friends were and where he could get support instead of people undermining him.

The problem was that he still had to talk to Bretton about it.

His friend would be pissed. They'd been working together for years, and Bretton had everything in place back at Lucifer's palace to make things easier. Moving would mean losing all of that, including the spies he had peppered around the palace and the infrastructure he used to solve many of their problems. He'd have to find a new palace, tell a bunch of high-placed demons that Lucifer was moving, and possibly deal with the fallout of him moving so close to one of the princes.

Lucifer was supposed to be impartial. He had to treat all the princes the same way, and he did most of the time. The princes treated him differently, though. Berith was the nicest and most honest, and they'd become true friends over time. The other princes either wanted to kill Lucifer and take his place or to manipulate him, and neither of those things made Lucifer want to be friends with them.

He didn't care what the princes or anyone else thought of him. They'd try to argue the move, but he wouldn't listen to them. If they didn't like what he was doing, they could try to stop him, but no one would be able to. He was the king, and no one had authority over him, not even Bretton.

Or at least, that was what Lucifer was trying to convince himself of.

He needed allies to make Bretton see that this was the best thing for both of them. Bretton might not like the idea right now, but surely, he'd eventually see that not having to deal with people wanting to kill Lucifer or undermine him every day would make his life easier, too. There was one person who would be able to convince Bretton of this more than Lucifer, and Lucifer was looking for him right now.

Mel.

The human was adorable and smart, and Lucifer had to believe that Bretton would listen to him. If anything, he'd do so out of respect for Berith, and then, he'd fall half in love with Mel and agree to whatever the human suggested.

Usually, Berith's consort could be found in the suite he shared with Berith or in his classroom. Lucifer had visited the children the other day, and they'd been as awkward as they were adorable. Some had been afraid of him, while others were excited. Lucifer had especially liked the little girl who'd climbed on his back without hesitation. She hadn't seen a reason to be afraid of him, and he loved that. Even most adults were afraid of him, and it wasn't always easy to deal with the knowledge of that. It wasn't that Lucifer wanted people to be afraid of him. He just wanted to be respected and obeyed, but it felt like it was too much to ask most days.

He turned a corner and stopped when he saw the demon coming toward him.

Yakim.

They'd kept their distance, and Lucifer was annoyed. He still didn't understand why he felt so drawn to Yakim, but after thinking about it, he'd decided it didn't matter. He was attracted to Yakim, and that was all there was to it. He didn't need a reason to be and was fine with not having one. He just knew that Yakim was handsome, fascinating, a hard worker, and loved by Berith and his family. That was enough to tell Lucifer that he was a good person and worthy of Lucifer's crush on him.

He was one more reason Lucifer wanted to stick around. He didn't often feel the way he did when it came to Yakim. He didn't allow himself to have crushes on people who lived at the palace because, more often than not, they used it against him. Over the decades, he'd learned to ignore his emotions and school his expressions, but he found himself feeling unguarded when Yakim was involved. Even more so, Lucifer didn't *want* to be guarded around him. He didn't want to hide his emotions or what he wanted.

He just wanted Yakim in any way he could have him.

There might never be anything between them, and Lucifer wasn't planning to move just because of Yakim, but being able to see him as often as he wanted would definitely be a plus. Before doing that, though, he'd have to make Yakim want to see him. He had the impression that Yakim had been avoiding him, but he wasn't sure. Maybe Yakim was just working.

There was only one way to find out.

They were going to cross paths unless one of them used one of the doors that opened in the hallway. Lucifer wasn't going to, which left Yakim. Lucifer stopped walking and watched him, knowing that Yakim had to be aware that he was there. He was good at his job.

By the time Yakim reached him, Lucifer felt like he was about to jump out of his skin. He grinned at the demon, but instead of smiling back, Yakim bowed at him and kept his gaze on the floor.

"Your Highness," he murmured.

Lucifer didn't like that. He might be the king, but he didn't want the people he liked to use his honorifics. To them, he just wanted to be Lucifer.

"Didn't I already tell you to call me Lucifer?"

"It doesn't feel right, your Highness. You're the king."

"And if your king tells you to do something, don't you want to do it?"

Yakim appeared nonplussed by the question. The answer should be that he'd do whatever Lucifer asked, but it was clear he also didn't want to stop calling him by his honorifics. Maybe Yakim thought keeping Lucifer at arm's length was easier if he used the honorifics. That way, they weren't just Yakim and Lucifer. They were a bodyguard and a king, and Yakim could believe they couldn't work together like that.

Lucifer knew better. Most demons didn't care about things like that beyond what they could gain from such a relationship. He and Yakim being together would put Yakim in danger, but he could defend himself. Really, he was the perfect guy for Lucifer.

If only Lucifer could convince him of that.

Yakim bowed again. "Of course, Lucifer. Is there anything I can do for you?"

There was so much he could do for Lucifer, but Lucifer couldn't ask for it.

Or could he?

Yakim felt like he was playing with fire. Had he really asked Lucifer what he could do for him? He suspected he knew the answer to that question. There was a reason Lucifer had been watching him, and it probably wasn't because he was trying to understand what kind of demon species were in Yakim's family. There was only one reason someone watched you the way he did, and it wasn't genealogy.

The thought that Lucifer wanted him made Yakim's stomach churn in the best way. He wanted Lucifer, too, even though it was a dangerous feeling. He shouldn't want the king of Hell in his bed. He should respect him and keep his distance, but it had been impossible to do. Something about Lucifer drew Yakim and everyone else in, and Yakim was incapable of resisting.

He wasn't sure he wanted to anymore.

It was foolish. There could never be anything between them, and not only because Lucifer was the king. Soon, he'd be going back to his palace, leaving Yakim behind. Whatever might have happened between them would be a thing of the past, and he'd soon forget about Yakim. Was this really what Yakim wanted? To be one more person the king of Hell had bedded before forgetting about him?

Yakim's past answer would have been no, but recently he'd found himself thinking about what it would be like. Besides, maybe Lucifer wouldn't forget about him. He didn't seem like the kind of demon who would do something like that, even though it was what Yakim had believed initially.

The king was very different from what Yakim had expected. He wasn't cold and haughty. He didn't look at everyone like they weren't worth spending time with them. He didn't rule with cruelty and fear. Every time Yakim had seen him talk to one of the servants, Lucifer had been respectful. He'd spoken to them as if they were his equals, and there was no way he was faking it because he did it even when no one else was around.

Yakim should know, since he'd been spying on the king.

He didn't do it often. He still spent most of his time with Mel, but when Mel was with Berith, Yakim and Roque had free time. Usually, Yakim would get something to eat or spend time in his room, but lately, he'd been tracking the king's path through the palace. He'd talked to the servants and the other people who dealt with him, and they all said the same thing.

The king was nice.

He was proving impossible to resist. As far as Yakim was concerned, Lucifer was more than nice. He was sweet but strong, didn't hesitate to help people, and stood his ground when he asked for something. He never forgot who and what he was, but he didn't use it against people or to gain things.

He could have. Getting Yakim into his bed would have been easy enough if he'd pushed for it. Initially, Yakim wouldn't have felt like he could say no. Berith would have intervened if he'd known, but Yakim wouldn't have gone to him if Lucifer had forced his way into his bed. He wouldn't have wanted his prince to be in trouble with the king.

But Lucifer had never done anything like that. He'd watched him from afar, making it clear to him and everyone else that he was interested. That was all there had been to it, though. He hadn't pushed, not even to talk to Yakim. Even now, Yakim knew that Lucifer would step aside if he said he had to go.

He didn't *want* to go. He was tired of resisting this, and even though he knew that Lucifer would leave soon, he wanted to see what it would be like to have the full focus of the king of Hell. He already knew Lucifer would be good to him. He was good to everyone.

Lucifer groaned. "Do you really have to say it like that?"

Yakim bowed again. "I apologize."

Lucifer shook his head. "Don't. This is a *me* problem, not a *you* problem. I'm surprised to see you on your own."

"The consort is spending time with the prince."

Lucifer grinned. "So you're telling me I shouldn't visit Berith's office right now."

Yakim almost smiled back. "Unless you want to interrupt them, I'd wait for a bit."

"What about you, Yakim? What will you be doing until Mel needs you again?"

"I was headed to my room to get some rest."

"Oh. I shouldn't keep you, then. If you need rest, I want you to get it."

He stepped aside, and Yakim knew that he could just walk away. But he was tired of resisting all of this. He was tired of acting as if Lucifer wasn't one of the nicest people he'd ever met. "I can go as soon as I help you with whatever you need help with."

Lucifer stared at Yakim. "I was actually looking for Mel, but since you're telling me he's busy, it'll have to wait."

"So you don't need me for anything?" Yakim pushed slightly. He didn't want to be more obvious than he already was, and he hoped Lucifer would understand what he was asking without saying the words.

He wasn't sure he understood what he was asking. Maybe if Lucifer would give him a chance? A chance at what, though?

No, this was stupid. He needed to leave Lucifer alone before either of them got hurt.

But it was too late. Yakim had given in, and Lucifer had noticed. He surged forward and grabbed Yakim's shoulder with one hand while he buried the fingers of his other hand in Yakim's hair. He pulled him forward, and their lips pressed together.

Yakim sucked in a breath. He'd imagined this moment many times but hadn't thought it would happen in a hallway where anyone could see them. Even though they shouldn't do this here, he grabbed Lucifer's waist and plastered their bodies together. He turned them and pressed Lucifer's back against the wall as Lucifer opened his mouth to him.

Lucifer was giving him all the control, and that stoked the fire in Yakim. He could never have imagined that the king of Hell would give him control over anything, let alone his body. Maybe he was doing so because he thought Yakim needed it, or perhaps because he enjoyed it. Whatever the reason, Yakim wanted to give him everything he wished for.

The kiss wasn't sweet and gentle. It wasn't soft and slow. It was all-consuming, almost as if he and Lucifer were trying to devour each other. Their lips were smashed together, their tongues tangled, and Yakim's entire world was reduced to the man in his arms for just a few moments.

The sound of a door opening in the distance startled him. He quickly staggered back, hitting the wall as he stared at the king.

Lucifer had never looked so sexy. His cheeks were flushed, he was panting, and he had one of his hands raised as if reaching for Yakim. Maybe that was what he was doing, but Yakim couldn't give in again. He wasn't sorry for what had just happened but couldn't let it happen again.

He pushed away from the wall and stiffly bowed to Lucifer. "My king," he murmured before turning around and almost running down the hallway.

He expected Lucifer to try to stop him, but he didn't say a word. When Yakim risked looking back when he reached the end of the hallway, he saw that Lucifer was still in the same position. His hand was down now, but he was against the wall as if he needed the support and was still staring at Yakim.

Yakim turned the corner, and Lucifer disappeared.

CHAPTER SIX

Yakim was back to ignoring Lucifer. Lucifer wasn't surprised, even though he was dismayed. The kiss had been the hottest thing that had happened to him in a long time, and he desperately wanted a repeat, but he didn't want to spook Yakim any more than he already had. If Lucifer was going to have a chance with him, he needed to allow Yakim to do this on his own terms.

The problem was that Yakim's terms seemed to be that he'd ignore Lucifer and that Lucifer should ignore him. Lucifer was willing to do a lot of things for Yakim, but not that. If Yakim wanted to ignore him, that was fine, but Lucifer wouldn't change his behavior. He'd been watching him since he'd arrived, and he still was, even though he was sure people had noticed.

He didn't care. Berith trusted the people who worked for him, and Lucifer trusted Berith. He didn't think anyone at the palace would use what they saw against him or Yakim, but even if they tried, Yakim could defend himself better than most. He'd been trained for it, and while Lucifer had never seen him use his training, he had no doubt that Yakim was lethal.

"All right, I've had enough," Bretton snapped.

Lucifer blinked at him. The suite of rooms that Berith had assigned to Lucifer had an office, and Lucifer and Bretton were sitting there working. Bretton was working, anyway. Lucifer had been daydreaming about Yakim, feeling like an excited teenager who'd discovered their sexuality for the first time. He was downright giddy, which wasn't like him.

"What is it?" he asked Bretton.

Bretton glared. "Don't tell me you don't know what I'm talking about. You're not focused. I had to insist on getting you to sit down and work, but you're not working. You're thinking about *him*."

Lucifer couldn't deny it. He didn't even have to ask who was the *him* Bretton was talking about. They both knew Lucifer's thoughts had been on Yakim since he'd arrived at the palace.

But Bretton was doing his job, and Lucifer should do his. It didn't matter that he was focused on Yakim. Bretton and Hell needed him, and he couldn't ignore that.

He straightened his back and cleared his throat. "I apologize."

Bretton shook his head. He still looked angry, but Lucifer was sure he'd get over it once he started paying attention.

"What's going on in your head?" Bretton asked. He put down his tablet and leaned forward. "And I'm asking as a friend, not as your personal assistant."

"You wouldn't believe me if I said nothing, would you?"

Bretton snorted. "I know you too well. I also know what's on your mind, but I don't understand. No one has ever caught your attention like he has. What's so different about him? As far as I know, you've barely even talked to him, let alone anything else. You shouldn't be so obsessed with someone you barely know."

He was right, but Lucifer couldn't explain it. What was it about Yakim that drew him in so fully?

Lucifer suspected it was a mix of things. Yakim was incredibly handsome, but he was also competent. He was gentle with Mel but tough when it came to defending him. He didn't hesitate to place himself between Mel and whatever he considered a danger. He hadn't tried to manipulate Lucifer in any way, even when he'd realized that Lucifer was watching him. He could have used that to his advantage. It wouldn't have been hard for him to seduce Lucifer like countless others had before.

But he wouldn't have been Yakim if he'd done that. Lucifer wouldn't have wanted him as badly as he did.

He leaned back in his chair and tilted his head to stare at the ceiling. "He doesn't want anything from me."

There was a moment of silence as if Bretton was thinking about it. "Everyone else does," he said eventually.

Lucifer nodded. "Almost everyone else. You don't want anything from me, and neither does Berith. Every demon I've slept with has tried to obtain something from me or manipulate me, though. I can't remember the last time I felt comfortable and like I didn't have to be on my guard when I was intimate with someone. I feel like Yakim could give me that. He could have used the fact that I've been watching him to his advantage, but he hasn't. I don't think he ever would, either. He's strong and capable, and all of that is highly appealing."

Lucifer risked glancing at Bretton. He didn't like the pity he could see in his friend's gaze, but maybe he was to be pitied.

"Have you tried talking to him?" Bretton asked.

"He's been avoiding me." Lucifer didn't tell Bretton that it had worsened since he and Yakim kissed. That was something only he and Yakim needed to know.

"I think you have your answer, then. He's remarkable, but if he doesn't want anything to do with you, you need to let it go." He hesitated. "Maybe it would be a good idea to go back to the palace. I don't think staying and seeing him daily is helping you. I know you don't want to go back and that you wish you could stay with your friends, and I understand, but it's not possible."

Lucifer opened his mouth to mention finding a palace in

the area, but one hard look from Bretton was enough for him to snap his mouth shut.

Bretton wasn't wrong. Lucifer was needed at his palace, and even though he still dreamed of finding a place here, maybe it was supposed to stay a dream. Moving so many people would be complicated, maybe even impossible. Lucifer couldn't do so just because he didn't like his palace.

"You have to keep control of your family and the other people at the palace," Bretton explained as if Lucifer didn't already know that. "You've been away long enough, maybe even too long. Your father and your sister have been talking to many people, and while everyone seems to be on your side so far, it won't last if you don't make an appearance. We already know a group of people wants to kill you. Don't give them the upper hand because you think you've fallen in love with a demon who doesn't want you."

Bretton had gone straight to the point, and it hurt. Lucifer had believed he'd found the one person who would want him for who he was rather than what he was. Maybe he had, but it was clear that Yakim didn't see him that way. He'd had many opportunities and enough time to think about what he wanted and take it, but he was avoiding Lucifer.

Lucifer had his answer.

He didn't want to go back, but he didn't have a choice. He often didn't, even though he was the king of Hell. He'd learned to deal with that and make his peace with it, and he would learn again once he went back.

"You can start organizing everything to go back," he told Bretton. His voice sounded dead, and that was how he felt inside.

"Lucifer—" Bretton began.

Lucifer shook his head. "You're right. I need to remember who and what I am and stop dreaming about what I could have had if my life had been different. My life isn't different.

I'm the king of Hell, and that won't ever change unless someone kills me."

"Don't talk that way."

Lucifer grinned. "Don't worry. I'm not planning to let anyone close enough to kill me. I'll be on the throne for years,
and I'll change Hell."

It wasn't like he had anything else to focus on — or anyone
else.

Yakim needed to talk to someone. He felt like he might explode if he didn't, and while that wouldn't be the case, what
had happened with Lucifer weighed heavily on his mind.

What was he supposed to do about the kiss? He'd been
avoiding the king since then, but he didn't think it was the
right way to do this. The problem was that he didn't know if
there was a right way, or if it existed, what it was. Avoiding
Lucifer didn't seem like a good idea, but what else could Yakim do?

The mature thing to do would be to talk to the king. Yakim
could tell him that what had happened between them was a
mistake and would never happen again. It wouldn't be
wrong, anyway. There were rumors that Lucifer was planning to return to his palace soon, so it was probably best that
Yakim hadn't let things go too far between them.

Why did he regret not dragging Lucifer into the nearest
bedroom if it was a good thing?

He didn't have an answer. He didn't think he wanted to
have one because he was afraid of what it would be. Maybe it
didn't feel like a mistake because it wasn't. Lucifer and Yakim
were different and felt like they didn't belong together, but
the same could be said for Berith and Mel, yet they were very
much in love and making it work.

Yakim didn't fool himself into thinking that he would ever

be Lucifer's consort, but he didn't want to be. He just wanted to be with Lucifer, which in itself was odd because they barely knew each other.

They hadn't talked more than a handful of times. They hadn't had much opportunity, and when they had, Yakim had avoided it. But he'd watched Lucifer, maybe as much as Lucifer had watched him. He'd seen the king with Mel and with the children. He'd listened to him work with Bretton and Berith.

Lucifer was nothing like the monster a lot of demons believed he was. He was a good ruler, and if he'd been anyone else, Yakim would have fallen all over himself to get him.

But Lucifer wasn't anyone else. He was the king of Hell, and that was much too big for Yakim.

"You have to stop doing that," Roque whispered as he bumped their shoulders together, bringing Yakim back to the present.

He straightened his back and looked around the room. How could he not have noticed that the children had left? They might be tiny, but they made enough noise to rival a group of fighting demons. Normally, it would have been impossible for Yakim not to notice them leave.

Yakim gave Roque a tight nod and turned his attention back to Mel, who was putting away the last things he'd used during the class. He moved quickly and efficiently, and soon they were ready to leave.

But they didn't. Instead, Mel hopped onto his desk, sitting in between books and pencils. His gaze pinned Yakim down, and Yakim sucked in a breath, waiting to find out what was about to happen.

"I would never force you to talk about anything you don't feel ready for, but I'm worried," Mel said.

"You don't have to be," Yakim assured him. "I might be distracted, but I would never leave you unprotected. Besides, it won't happen again. I swear."

Mel looked almost disappointed. "I don't care about my protection. I've always thought that Berith assigning me two bodyguards was overkill, but I won't be changing his mind, so I haven't tried much. Besides, I like the two of you, which is why I'm worried about you."

"You have no reason to be." Maybe Yakim would sound convincing enough for Mel to believe him.

Mel wasn't impressed. "Better liars than you have tried fooling me, and they haven't succeeded. If you don't want to talk to me, that's fine. I understand we're in an odd position since you work for Berith and me. You need to talk to someone, though. This is hurting you."

Yakim sighed. It would be weird to talk to Mel, but he knew Mel would do his best to help him, and in the end, that was what mattered. They were friends.

"It's Lucifer," Yakim admitted. "He's been watching me, and I've been watching him, and I like him, but I know nothing can come out of it. We kissed in the hallway the other day, and it was incredible, but I've been ignoring him since then, and I've heard rumors that he's leaving, so it's for the best. I guess it's distracting me, and I'm sorry about that, but I'm sure that as soon as he leaves, I'll go back to normal."

The words fell out of Yakim's mouth, and Yakim was unable to stop them. He couldn't remember the last time he'd said so much so quickly, and he snapped his mouth shut.

Roque was watching him with wide eyes, but Mel seemed almost sorry. It was an expression Yakim never wanted to see aimed at him, but it wasn't like he could do anything about it. If their roles were reversed, he'd be sorry for himself, too.

"You kissed the king of Hell?" Roque blurted out.

Of course that was all he'd gotten from everything Yakim had said. "He kissed me. I just didn't push him away."

"Because you didn't want to or because you felt you

couldn't?" Mel asked.

Yakim understood why he was asking, but it was ridiculous. "He'd never force me into doing anything, let alone that. I *wanted* him to kiss me, and I enjoyed it much more than I should have."

Roque snickered. "I bet you did. I mean, he's sexy."

He was, but Yakim couldn't allow himself to think about Lucifer. He was trying to get over him, not to fall for him even more.

"So you're sure he didn't force you in any way?" Mel asked.

"I promise that he didn't. He kissed me, and I kissed him back because I wanted to. I stopped things before they could get too far, and I don't know what to do. It would be best to stay away from him, wouldn't it?"

"I would," Roque piped in. "He might be hot, but he's also fucking scary. Honestly, I wouldn't want to be in your place. I wouldn't know what to do, either, except run for the hills. The guy is powerful, Yakim. He could crush you with one thought."

Lucifer could, so Yakim didn't even try to deny it. But he'd never been afraid of him. Lucifer was powerful. He had to be, to keep the palace and Hell under control. He could also be ruthless and didn't hesitate to hurt people if they deserved it or if it was needed to keep others safe. That wasn't all there was to him, and Yakim was equally attracted to both sides of him.

He liked that Lucifer could be gentle and sweet but also that he was uncompromising when it came to his job and his protection of Hell. That was what had pulled Yakim toward him initially. Lucifer was such a confusing puzzle, full of contrasts, and Yakim wanted to pull him apart and put *them* back together. He wanted to learn more about Lucifer and to find the soft heart he had to hide under a hard exterior.

Shit. Yakim was in trouble.

"What do you want?" Mel asked. "Forget about everything else. Forget that he's the king of Hell and that you live here, and he doesn't. What would you want if it were just the two of you, Yakim and Lucifer?"

That was easy. "I want him. But I can't forget that he's the king of Hell, and I'm a bodyguard. It's part of who we are."

"Maybe, but maybe not. Look at Berith and me. I'm human, and people would never have thought I could survive here, let alone become Berith's consort. Yet I'm here, and I'm thriving. I wouldn't have any of this if I hadn't been willing to give Berith and me a chance, and while I'm not saying you need to do the same, I'd like it if you kept an open mind. Lucifer is the king of Hell, and I can't even begin to imagine how awkward and scary your position is, but if by the end of it, you can have what Berith and I have, then maybe it would be worth it."

He was right. It didn't matter that he and Berith were different. They fit together and made it work in a way Yakim had seldom seen in Hell. There was no way to know if things would be the same for him and Lucifer, but they wouldn't know if they didn't try.

The problem was that Lucifer would leave eventually, and Yakim couldn't go with him.

CHAPTER SEVEN

"Go. I'll be fine," Mel said as he pushed Yakim toward the door.

Yakim hesitated and looked at Roque. Their job was to stay with Mel all day, every day. When he moved around the palace, they were his shadows. They weren't supposed to take breaks in the middle of the day, yet Mel was pushing them to do just that.

"We should stay with you," Roque said.

Mel shook his head. "I'm in my rooms. I'll be fine. There are guards outside, and Berith will have lunch with me here today."

Yakim frowned. "You're not eating with everyone else?"

"I'm not sure we'll be eating at all."

Yakim's body flushed hot with embarrassment when he realized what Mel was talking about. He didn't want to think about his prince and Mel doing that. He certainly didn't want to be there when it happened, and he didn't think Berith would be happy if he and Roque were still around when he arrived.

Yakim and Roque glanced at each other again, and Roque hurried out the door.

"We'll see you after lunch," Yakim said.

Mel's smile was gentle. "Take this opportunity to relax a bit, all right? You've been on the edge for a while."

He didn't say that Yakim had been on the edge since Lucifer had arrived at the palace, but he wouldn't be wrong if he had. That *was* how long Yakim had been on edge.

He hadn't known what to think of the king of Hell when Lucifer had stared at him every chance he had, and he still didn't know what to think of him now that Lucifer had kissed him. He should probably talk to the king and ask for an explanation, but he wasn't sure that would be a good idea. It might give him peace of mind, but it might also get him killed.

Yakim left Mel behind after making sure that Mel would lock the door behind him, and by the time he reached the hallway, Roque had vanished. He'd no doubt decided to take advantage of the free time they had to go to lunch or meet whoever he was sleeping with at the moment. Yakim might have done the same, but he wasn't sleeping with anyone.

His mind flashed to Lucifer, and he scowled. He and Lucifer weren't sleeping together. Just the thought of him and the king together like that made him want to roll his eyes and run away at the same time. There was no way Lucifer wanted him that way.

But he'd kissed him.

It hadn't been a friendly kiss. It had been a real kiss that wouldn't be odd between lovers. What had Lucifer meant by it?

Probably nothing. Lucifer was set to leave, and Yakim had heard rumors that it wouldn't be long before he did. Even if something might have been growing between them, they couldn't give in to it. Lucifer wasn't here to stay. He was the king, while Yakim was nothing more than a bodyguard. Just the thought of them together was ridiculous.

Yakim had too much energy to sit down to eat lunch, so he headed for the garden instead. It would be quiet at this time of day, and as long as he avoided the private garden that opened on the suite Berith and Mel shared, he'd be fine. He had no intention of spying on them and seeing things that would scar him for life.

He stayed far away from the private garden the prince's

family used and instead chose a smaller one. Servants were allowed here, but they seldom visited. There wasn't much to see. Not many people appreciated plants, but Yakim didn't mind them. Sometimes he felt more at peace here than surrounded by people. The plants were silent, and it was soothing.

Yakim even had a favorite spot in the garden. It was out of the way so that even if someone walked through, they wouldn't see him. There was a stone bench surrounded by tall trees and rocks where Yakim could sit and hide for a while. He couldn't spend as much time as he wanted there today, but it would be better than nothing.

He crossed the garden and headed toward his hiding spot. He was almost there when he heard footsteps behind him, and he almost groaned. He was sure someone was looking for him to tell him that Mel needed something or other, so he plastered a cool expression on his face and turned.

Only to see Lucifer.

Like always, he wore a black suit. His hair was braided and hung over one shoulder, but as Yakim watched, Lucifer huffed and pushed it behind his back. He raised his hand and waved at Yakim, and Yakim stared, wondering if the king expected him to wave back. That thought was too ridiculous for him to give it more than a fleeting thought, and he hadn't waved back by the time Lucifer reached him.

"I thought that was you," Lucifer said.

Yakim arched a brow. "I doubt there are many demons at the palace who look like me."

"Probably not." Lucifer glanced around. He seemed awkward, which wasn't like him. Lucifer wasn't the kind of demon who shuffled his feet and avoided looking Yakim in the eyes. He was the kind of demon who faced whatever was coming at him head-on.

But not today.

"Was there something you wanted, your Highness?" Ya-kim asked, straightening his spine and bowing lightly. Lucifer might have kissed him, but he was still the king of Hell.

Lucifer groaned. "I hate it when you call me that."

"What else should I call you, your Highness?"

"By my name."

"I'm not sure I can do that."

Lucifer groaned. "I've made a mess out of this." He cleared his throat and stood taller. "I wanted to apologize for kissing you without your consent. I shouldn't have, especially considering who both of us are. You probably felt you couldn't push me away, but I want you to know that I wouldn't have hurt you in any way if you had."

Yakim realized that from the outside, that was what it might have looked like, but it couldn't be further from the truth. He hadn't pushed Lucifer away because he'd been enjoying the kiss, not because he'd felt he couldn't.

"You don't have to apologize," he said.

"I really do. It's not like me to do something like that without asking first, and I hate that I did it to you, of all people."

Yakim nodded curtly. "Well, thank you, but I didn't kiss you back because I thought I didn't have a choice."

Lucifer cocked his head. "Why did you?"

Yakim had a choice. He could be honest and see what happened, or he could lie so Lucifer wouldn't try to kiss him again. That would be the smartest choice. Lucifer would leave soon. Once he did, Yakim would be left with a handful of nothing.

But if Lucifer was leaving soon, this might be the only occasion Yakim had to do this. Was he ready to waste it? He'd never have another opportunity to kiss Lucifer again.

He looked around, but they were alone, surrounded only by trees and plants. His hidden spot wasn't far, and if something was going to happen between them, it was the best place for it. No one would walk in on them.

Yakim sucked in a breath. He knew what he wanted but wasn't sure he'd have the guts to do so.

"Yakim?" Lucifer asked.

Yakim snapped. He didn't want to have regrets. He grabbed Lucifer's hand, ignored his muffled squeak, and pulled him toward his hiding spot. Thankfully, Lucifer didn't argue or try to pull away. He followed Yakim until Yakim stopped by the stone bench and turned to face him. He cupped the king's face with both his hands and lowered his head to kiss him.

It was as glorious as it had been the first time. Yakim wasn't surprised. He knew what to expect this time, and he planned to enjoy every second of it.

He swiped his tongue over Lucifer's lips, and they opened for him. Lucifer pressed close, wrapping his arms around Yakim's neck to hold them in place as if he expected him to run. He might, but not right now.

Their tongues touched, and Yakim groaned. Lucifer was driving him nuts without even trying. Yakim wanted much more than a kiss, but he didn't dare ask for it.

He ran his hands up and down Lucifer's back. When he reached the top of Lucifer's buttocks, he hesitantly pushed a finger under the king's belt. He found the edge of the king's shirt and bunched it up, his fingertip grazing skin.

Lucifer shuddered in Yakim's arms. For a second, Yakim expected him to tell him to fuck off and stop touching him, but that wasn't what happened.

Lucifer pushed him backward. Yakim knew where the bench was and managed to land on it without making a fool of himself. He didn't have time to ask Lucifer what was happening. The king scrambled onto Yakim's lap, straddling his hips as he reached for his belt. He continued kissing him as he unfastened his pants and took his cock out, and Yakim couldn't have stopped even if he'd wanted to. Lucifer was all-consuming, wrapped around him. At the moment, he was Yakim's entire world. There was nothing beyond the two of them and this stone bench.

Lucifer traced a path down Yakim's jaw and his throat, pressing kisses to his skin and nibbling on it. Yakim felt him pull on his pants, and Lucifer unzipped them when he didn't stop him. Yakim sucked in a breath at the feeling of the king's fingers on his hard cock. He had no idea what Lucifer had in mind, but he trusted him, something he was surprised to realize.

All thoughts flew out the window when Lucifer wrapped his hand around both their cocks. Lucifer's skin was warm and silky. His cock pulsed lightly, and Yakim answered in kind. Lucifer's hands were slightly rougher, but it added to the pleasure. Lucifer was a study in contrast—a hard king but a gentle soul. He wanted people to be happy but wouldn't hesitate to hurt anyone who deserved it.

And he wanted Yakim.

Lucifer bit hard on Yakim's neck. Yakim jerked back, but Lucifer wouldn't have any of it. He continued nibbling on Yakim's skin as Yakim grabbed his ass with both hands, hauling him closer. He made a whining sound when Lucifer's hold on their cocks tightened. He didn't think he'd ever felt anything more arousing than what he felt now, and he wanted more of it, yet at the same time, he was unwilling to let go of the king.

"You're so beautiful," Lucifer muttered. "And I want you so much. I didn't think this would happen."

Yakim hadn't thought it would happen, either, and he didn't know what to say, so instead of answering, he dug his fingertips into Lucifer's hair and held his head in place as he kissed him again. Lucifer moaned, and the rhythm of his hand faltered, but not for long.

Yakim did his best to give Lucifer pleasure. He touched

and kissed him everywhere he could, moving around the clothing Lucifer still wore. The king's body was soft and hard at the same time, and it made Yakim yearn for so much more.

He grinned against Lucifer's lips when he felt the king shudder in his arms, and a warm wetness hit his cock. Lucifer's thick cock jerked as he came, and the added slickness, paired with the twisting movement Lucifer made with the hand he still had around their cocks pushed Yakim over the edge. He clung to Lucifer as he came and buried his face against Lucifer's neck.

He couldn't remember the last time he'd felt so much pleasure, but unfortunately, the warm sensation didn't last long.

What had he done?

For a moment, Lucifer was in heaven, which wasn't something a demon could often say. Unfortunately for him, it didn't last nearly long enough.

Yakim's body was loose and relaxed against Lucifer's for just a few moments after he came. Then his back tensed, and Lucifer knew it was over. The problem was that he was straddling Yakim's lap. That meant that if Yakim wanted to run, like Lucifer suspected he did, he'd have to dump him to the ground. Yakim would never do something like that, but Lucifer could feel his body almost trembling with the need to run, and he didn't want to force him to stay if he didn't want to. It was obvious he hadn't planned what had happened between them and that he didn't know how to deal with it.

He wasn't the only one. Lucifer had no idea why this had happened, and he needed time to wrap his mind around it. He'd thought he didn't have a chance with Yakim, that it was time for him to give up the dream and return to his palace, but Yakim had handed him what he'd been dreaming of since the first time he saw him. Lucifer hoped it wasn't just physical, but he couldn't be sure.

Sighing, he swung one of his legs back and to the side. He slid off Yakim's lap and landed on the stone bench next to him. His pants were still undone, his cock out, and it was uncomfortable, to say the least. Anyone could walk in on them at any moment, and they'd get an eyeful. Lucifer was lucky he'd managed to ditch his bodyguards.

Lucifer didn't want to get dressed while dirty, but Yakim didn't seem to have that problem. As soon as Lucifer was off him, he jumped to his feet and scrambled to cover himself. Lucifer was slower, and by the time he was done, Yakim was bowing to him, then practically running away.

Lucifer watched him go and resisted the temptation to go after him. He wanted to know what this meant, but he wouldn't get his answer if he pushed too hard at the wrong moment. Yakim probably didn't know yet, anyway. He needed time to wrap his mind around it and make decisions, and Lucifer would give him that.

Yakim suddenly stopped moving. Lucifer held his breath, hoping he was coming back. Maybe they could go to Lucifer's suite for a few hours, or if Yakim had to go back to work, even half an hour would do.

Yakim didn't turn to look at Lucifer. "This was a one-time thing," he said.

Lucifer frowned. "Why?"

Yakim finally turned, but he still didn't look at Lucifer. He kept his attention on the ground next to the bench, which made Lucifer want to sit in the dirt so Yakim would *have* to look at him.

"Because we don't make sense. I'm a bodyguard here, and I have no intention of leaving Mel and Berith, and you're the king of Hell and live in your palace. What just happened can't happen again."

"Not even if we both want it?" That was the answer Lucifer needed. As long as they were both okay with this, he'd do whatever he could to ensure they could experience this again. He wasn't a quitter. A little hardship wouldn't scare him into letting go of Yakim.

"You'd want to?" Yakim sounded like he couldn't quite believe it.

"I would love to. I like you, Yakim. I know things are complicated, but it doesn't mean we can't make it work."

"I like you, too," Yakim whispered.

When Lucifer saw his shoulders square and his back go ramrod straight, he knew he'd lost. As much as Yakim clearly wanted this, he would resist. It wasn't a surprise, but it was disappointing.

"We both need to forget about this," Yakim continued. "It shouldn't have happened at all, but it did, and we'll have to live with that."

"You talk as if what we did was horrible, but it's not. We're both consenting adults, and no one will care if they find out about it."

"I will. I already told you I can't follow you back to your palace, and I don't think you want me to. I was probably nothing more than a bit of fun to finish your visit here on a high, and that's fine with me. I just don't think I can stand doing it again before you leave."

Lucifer wanted to yell at him to stop being an idiot, but he didn't get the opportunity. Yakim seemed to have realized that Lucifer would argue, so as soon as he was done speaking, he turned around and left. Once again, Lucifer was tempted to go after him, but instead, he thought about what he'd learned today.

Yakim found him attractive and wanted to sleep with him. More importantly, it sounded like this one time hadn't been enough and like the only reason they wouldn't do it again was that Yakim wasn't willing to compromise and leave the place he called home.

That was fine with Lucifer. He wasn't planning to take Yakim or anyone Lucifer cared about back to his palace. The place was full of enemies, and if he could, he'd never go back.

Maybe that was what he should do. He had put that dream away when he'd thought he didn't have a reason to move to the area, but now, he knew he did. Yakim wanted him but didn't want to leave his friends behind. He'd have to if he and Lucifer ended up together, but maybe he didn't have to go far. If he lived close by, he could still see Berith, Mel, and the rest of the people he cared about.

But he could do so from Lucifer's side.

Lucifer was convinced they could find a way to make this work. They'd both have to compromise, but he was ready to and hoped Yakim was, too. For now, he was trying to fool himself into believing there was nothing between them and that it had only been sex, but it hadn't been.

If they allowed the feelings between them to grow, they could have something special. Lucifer had thought he'd lost it before truly having it, and he was ready to do what he had to in order to make it work.

He'd show Yakim that he wasn't going anywhere and that Yakim wouldn't have to follow him, either. He'd find a palace in the area, maybe even open a permanent portal between the two so that Yakim could go back and forth whenever he wanted. He and Yakim would be happy.

Bretton, on the other hand, wouldn't be.

CHAPTER EIGHT

"You want me to do *what*?" Bretton asked.

Lucifer kept his chin high. He wasn't going to cower in front of his personal assistant. "I want you to find me a palace in the area. I want it to be close to this one so that I can visit whenever I want."

Bretton looked at him like he'd lost his mind. Maybe he had. He was doing this without even talking to Yakim about it, which might mean trouble and end in disaster. There was no way to know how Yakim would react when he found out Lucifer was doing this, but Lucifer would find out soon enough.

"You can already visit whenever you want. You just have to open a portal."

"We both know that's not the best idea. Besides, I don't want to live in the palace anymore. I never liked it, and it hasn't improved over the years."

Bretton leaned forward, his tablet forgotten on the table next to the armchair he was sitting in. "The palace is the seat of your power. It's where your ministers and all the demons important to your reign are. You can't ask them to move. Besides, do you know how much time and money it would take to move so many people here?"

"Are you saying it's impossible?"

Lucifer knew his friend. Bretton would never say something was impossible, and if he could show it wasn't, it would be even better. Lucifer hadn't dared him, but he knew Bretton would want to show him he could do it.

Bretton flopped back in his seat. "I don't believe you. We agreed to go back to the palace. You're needed there, and you can't avoid it."

"We can go back if you think it's necessary, do the work we need to do, then return here. I could even go back by myself, since I want you to find me a new palace as soon as possible."

"You're not going anywhere without me." Bretton's eyes were narrow, and his lips pressed into a scowl. "I can't believe you're doing this to me."

"I'm sure you can. You know me better than almost anyone else."

"You're right. I *can* believe it. I should have known you wouldn't let this go even after the bodyguard didn't give you the time of day." His eyes narrowed even more. "Is he the reason you're doing this?"

"In part," Lucifer admitted because lying would be useless. "I want to get to know him and see where things can go, but he's not the only reason. I want to move closer to Berith. You know he's one of my few friends, and I trust him with my life. I hate that we're so far apart and that it took him destroying a secret society in his palace for me to finally meet his consort. I like Mel, too, and I want to spend more time getting to know him better. I can see us becoming friends, and we have things in common that most other demons can't understand."

That included Bretton. No one would mistake him for a human, so he couldn't understand how good it felt to have someone know what it was like. Mel did, and even though their situations were different, Lucifer felt a certain kind of kinship with him. It was like, with Mel, Lucifer could let go of the king persona and be himself.

Nothing was calling Lucifer back to his palace, while everything told him to stay. Surely that had to count for something.

Bretton pinched the bridge of his nose and closed his eyes. "Let me get this straight. You want me to find you a palace and start the process of moving everyone and everything from your old palace to the new one. You want to do so because you wish to be closer to your friend and to the guy you're trying to sleep with."

Lucifer leaned back against the couch and glared at his friend. "Why are you saying it like that?"

"How else am I supposed to say it? It's what you're asking me to do."

"No. I'm asking you to find me a palace and start the process of moving everything and *some* of the people here. I don't want my enemies to come along. I want people who are on my side."

"And how am I supposed to know if they are? Should I ask them?"

"We both know you don't need to. You already know who my enemies are." That included Lucifer's father and his sister.

"I could have bad intel. I could make mistakes. There's no way to be sure of something like that."

"I trust you."

"What if you shouldn't? What if I make a mistake and you get hurt?"

This wasn't Lucifer's personal assistant speaking. It was his friend, so he reached out to Bretton, gently squeezing his knee. "I trust you," he repeated. "You only want what's best for me, and I know you'll do what you can so I can have it. What I need right now is to stay away from the palace permanently. I need a place to call home where I won't feel like an outsider or like demons are sizing me up for either marriage or murder. I don't expect you to understand, but I'm not going to change my mind."

"I know. We'll still have to go back, though, and you know that."

Lucifer did, but the knowledge that he'd return to Berith's palace soon would be enough to carry him through whatever he had to deal with there.

He grinned and leaned forward to smack a kiss on Bretton's cheek, then jumped to his feet. "I'm going to find Berith and tell him the good news."

"Take your bodyguards with you," Bretton ordered. "You've been leaving them behind, and I don't like it."

"They don't have to protect me against anyone in Berith's palace."

"Maybe not, but I'd feel better if I knew they were with you. Do it for me." Lucifer had a soft spot for him, and he was using it to his advantage.

Lucifer loved it.

When he walked through the door of the suite he was staying in, he gestured at the bodyguards standing guard by it. They'd come with him from the palace and didn't belong to Berith's people, but Lucifer trusted them as much as he trusted most people in his life. He doubted they'd hesitate if someone offered them a bunch of money to kill him, which was why he paid them extremely well.

"We're going to the prince's office," he explained as they walked.

The guest wing was mostly empty at this time of day. Everyone was working, and Lucifer had been, too, before leaving Bretton behind. Hopefully, Bretton was already looking into what needed to be done to move what needed to be moved and, more importantly, *who* needed to be moved.

They rounded a corner, and Lucifer could see the door out of the guest wing at the end of the hallway. He moved faster, eager to see Berith, but a weird, strangled sound behind him made him pause. He turned, his eyes widening at seeing one of his bodyguards stabbing the other in the throat.

"Step away from her," he ordered.

Barnum obeyed, which was a relief. The problem was that he turned his attention to Lucifer.

Lucifer doubted that Barnum had been paid to kill his fellow bodyguard, which meant he was here for Lucifer.

Lucifer glanced at Sahndra, who was holding herself up against the wall with one hand while the other clutched at her neck to try to stop the blood flow. Lucifer didn't know how long she had to live, but if he wanted a chance to save her, he needed to get rid of Barnum.

That wouldn't be a problem.

The sound of fighting was the first thing that told Yakim something was wrong. For a moment, he was confused. People weren't supposed to fight in the palace. What was happening?

He and Roque looked at each other. Roque stepped back toward Mel, grabbing his arm and pulling him in the direction of one of the rooms in the hallway they were walking along. Mel looked confused and attempted to pull away, but Roque didn't let go.

"What's going on?" Mel asked.

He sounded frightened, which wasn't what Yakim had been aiming for. "I don't know yet. I'm going to go see so we can be sure you're safe, all right? Stay with Roque."

Mel wrapped his arms around himself and nodded. He stared at Yakim for a few moments longer before finally following Roque willingly. Yakim waited until the two of them had disappeared through the nearest door before turning and rushing toward the sound of fighting.

He had to turn another two corners before finding the source of the noise. When he finally did, the first thing he saw was a bleeding demon slumped against the wall. He recognized her as one of Lucifer's bodyguards, and his eyes widened when he turned his attention to the fight in the middle of the hallway.

Lucifer's second bodyguard was holding a knife and trying to stab Lucifer. Lucifer kept moving around him, easily avoiding the hits. Every time he did, he hit the bodyguard somewhere, but while the bodyguard was bleeding, it wasn't enough to stop him.

Yakim hesitated. He needed to check whether the first bodyguard was alive, but his priority was Lucifer. As one of Berith's guards, his job was to protect the king of Hell. Even more so, he *wanted* to protect Lucifer.

But Lucifer didn't look like he needed help. As Yakim watched, he twirled toward a small table against the wall, grabbed the statue on top of it, and turned again to slam it down on top of his bodyguard's head. The demon had been trying to stab him in the stomach, but now he was the one who was hurt. He staggered back, blood dripping down his forehead, and seemed to realize he wouldn't win this. He was a mess, while Lucifer looked like he hadn't broken a sweat.

The bodyguard turned and started running. Unfortunately for him, he started running in Yakim's direction.

He was wounded and probably tired, and it only took a handful of seconds for Yakim to pin him down. He yanked the bodyguard's hands behind his back, ignoring his yelps, and made him drop the knife. He didn't have handcuffs, so he unhooked the bodyguard's belt and used that.

He only let go once he was sure the bodyguard wasn't a danger to Lucifer anymore.

"That was impressive," Lucifer drawled.

Yakim snorted. "You were, too."

"I won't deny that because it's true, but you weren't so bad yourself."

Yakim straightened and placed a foot on the bodyguard's back. He grabbed the demon's arm and rolled him to the side so he could look him in the eyes. "Who sent you?"

The bodyguard didn't answer, but Yakim hadn't expected he would. Lucifer had stepped away, but he quickly came back.

"The other bodyguard?" Yakim asked.

Lucifer looked sad as he shook his head. "She's dead." He turned his attention to the man who'd attacked him. "Why did you do it?"

The bodyguard glared at Lucifer, but he didn't say anything. When he grinned, Yakim knew something was wrong. He had no idea what, but when he saw the bodyguard chew something, he knew. He scrambled to pry open the bodyguard's mouth, but it was too late.

The demon fell back, his mouth open, foam coming out of it. Yakim didn't know what kind of poison he'd taken, but he was pretty sure that nothing would save him. The bodyguard had planned for this eventuality. He'd known he might be stopped while trying to kill Lucifer and decided to kill himself if it happened.

The bodyguard's body flopped on the floor, and when Yakim leaned down to check if he had a pulse, he didn't find anything. He was dead, too.

"What are the odds that he worked for the society?" Lucifer asked.

Yakim wasn't going to lie to him. "Pretty high."

Lucifer was shocked, and not just because one of his bodyguards had tried to kill him. He'd almost expected that. It wasn't the first time it happened, and no matter how carefully Bretton vetted the bodyguards, it wouldn't be the last. It was hard to find people Lucifer trusted with his life, so he was always on guard, and he was glad he had been today. He was sorry he'd lost Sahndra, too, but she'd known the risks of accepting this job.

"I can't believe this," Yakim snapped. "Your bodyguard? Who the fuck chose them? Didn't they look into these people's history?"

Lucifer wasn't sure how to take Yakim's angry reaction. "Bretton chose them, and you know him. Of course he looked into their past. He wouldn't have chosen them if there had been something wrong there."

Yakim pointed his finger at Barnum's body. "What do you call that if not wrong?"

If Lucifer had had doubts about Yakim's feelings for him before, he didn't anymore. It might not be a declaration of love, but it was as close as it could get to one, considering the circumstances. No matter what Yakim had said about them not having sex together again, it was clear he cared, which was enough to reassure Lucifer that he was doing the right thing.

"I'm fine," he promised.

"Only because of who you are."

"I suspect he attacked me only because of who I am, too. It comes with the territory, unfortunately. There's always going to be someone trying to kill me."

"Maybe, but your *bodyguard*?"

Someone called out, and Yakim answered. The sound of running indicated that people were coming, so Lucifer wasn't surprised when a bunch of guards came around the corner, their weapons out to defend him.

They were too late. Lucifer had defended himself.

"Get Reyni," Cam snapped at one of the guards.

"I don't think any of us here needs a healer," Lucifer told him. "I'm fine, and Sahndra and Barnum are dead."

"You're going to let him examine you," Yakim said.

His voice was still harsh and sent a shiver running down Lucifer's back. It shouldn't be this sexy, but it was.

"Are you ordering me to do that?" he asked carefully.

"I am."

"You do realize that I'm way above you in Hell's hierarchy, right?"

"I don't care. You can lock me in the dungeon if you want, but I won't go until I'm sure you don't have a scratch on you."

There could only be one reason for him to care so much, and that meant Lucifer was correct. Yakim's feelings for him were much more profound than mere attraction, and while he was resisting, Lucifer felt confident that he could woo him. He couldn't do that from his old palace, but as soon as possible, he'd move closer, and Yakim wouldn't be able to get rid of him.

"I'll get Mel and Roque," Yakim said. "I left them in a closet somewhere. I also need to contact Berith and Lon."

"I can do that," one of the guards said.

"Thanks, Mikal. I already had someone contact Reyni, so you don't have to worry about him."

Mikal's cheeks flushed, but whatever had caused his reaction didn't last long. He was all business as he took out a cell phone and used it to call Berith and his head of security.

Lucifer sighed. He probably needed to call Bretton, but he already knew his friend would freak out when he found out what had happened. He'd blame himself for choosing the wrong bodyguards, and Lucifer didn't want him to feel guilty. He didn't think that Barnum had been planning to kill him the entire time he'd worked for him. Initially, he'd been a pretty nice person.

But power and money could corrupt everyone, and it seemed the society had plenty of both. They'd had enough to pay off Lucifer's bodyguard and even to persuade him to kill himself when he failed. Lucifer was convinced that he knew who was behind this and who financed it more than ever. Normally, he'd attempt to prove it, but he was reaching the end of his patience.

He might just go straight to killing his father and his sister.

When Yakim had realized Lucifer was involved in the fight, he'd been terrified. He still was, even though the threat had been neutralized. His mind couldn't stop obsessing over what would have happened if Lucifer hadn't won the fight against his bodyguard. What if he'd been hurt? Worse, what if he'd been killed?

It was easy to imagine how bad things would have become in Hell, but that wasn't Yakim's main focus. That probably made him selfish, but he couldn't stop thinking about what would have happened to *him* if Lucifer had been killed.

He cared about Lucifer. He'd been trying to deny it, but he couldn't anymore. What just happened had shown him how important Lucifer was to him, and it would be useless to try to insist otherwise. Unless something changed, Yakim had to find a way to deal with it.

If Lucifer had been anyone else, it would have been easy. Yakim would have either given in and dated them or forgotten about them. He couldn't do either of those things with the king of Hell.

It wasn't because Lucifer was the king. That alone would make him unforgettable, but what made him so even more was who he was. Yakim had never expected Lucifer to be the way he was, and he didn't know how to forget him, even if he could. Being with him sounded impossible, but forgetting about him *was* impossible.

So what was he supposed to do? Especially after what happened between them in the garden, Yakim knew he needed to make a decision. Could he really ignore Lucifer until the king went back to his palace? Or would he give in like he had in the garden? How bad would things be if he did give in?

Yakim had to be honest with himself. He cared about Lucifer, and that wasn't going to change, especially if Lucifer decided to stay in the area. There were rumors that he was getting ready to go back to his palace, but there were other rumors that said he didn't want to and wanted to move closer. Yakim didn't know what it would take for Lucifer to permanently move closer to Berith, and he'd told himself it didn't matter, but he wasn't sure it didn't.

If Lucifer was moving, why was he doing it? Was it because he wanted to be closer to Berith? That would make sense from what Yakim knew about the relationship between the two. He could imagine that in Lucifer's position, it wasn't easy to make friends who wanted the best for him and weren't planning on using him. Berith was one of the few people Lucifer trusted, and it was clear watching the two of them that they cared greatly for each other. If Berith and Bretton were the only people Lucifer could trust, it would make sense for him to want to move closer to one of them and take the other along.

There was no way Lucifer was doing this for Yakim, or at least solely for him. Yakim still didn't understand how he'd caught the attention of the king of Hell, but he wasn't sure he'd be able to answer that question even if he asked Lucifer.

Maybe there wasn't an answer. Yakim couldn't explain why he was so attracted to the king, either. Sure, he could list all the things he liked about him, like how nice he was to Mel and the servants, how sweet he'd been with the children the other day, or how strong he was, but it was more than that. There was something that pulled Yakim in and made him yearn for Lucifer, and *that* was what he couldn't explain. He'd met more than one nice and sweet person and had never liked any of them more than he should.

But he liked Lucifer.

"What on earth happened here?" Berith asked as he strode

down the hallway toward them.

Lon was behind him, looking pissed. This wasn't his fault, even though he was the head of palace security, but if Yakim knew him, he'd take the attack personally.

"I'm fine," Lucifer promised. "One of my bodyguards killed the other and attacked me, then killed himself."

Berith stopped once he reached Lucifer and looked him up and down. "There's always drama around you."

"Nothing I can do about that," Lucifer murmured.

Berith clasped his shoulder. "Considering who you are, I don't expect you to. Still, it's a good thing you're leaving. I'll miss you, but I can't have people attacking each other in my hallways."

Yakim stepped closer to the wall, hoping no one would notice him. He should have left with Mel and Roque, but Lucifer had asked him to stay, and he couldn't say no to the king, especially when he didn't want to.

He'd known Lucifer was planning to leave, but he hadn't realized it would be so soon. He should have. He hadn't given Lucifer anything that would give him a reason to stay. They'd kissed and had a moment in the garden, but Yakim had been avoiding Lucifer since then, so it made sense that the king had decided that what had happened didn't mean anything.

Yakim wasn't going to beg him. Whatever happened between them was a one-time experience, just like he'd told Lucifer back in the garden. Yakim needed to remember that.

He was a simple bodyguard. He was good at his job, but he'd never be anything more than one of the people who protected Berith and his family. It was a good job, and he was proud of himself for rising so high in the hierarchy. He'd never do anything that might take him away from that role, especially not becoming the king's consort. He didn't want that, and there was no way to know how people would react if Yakim was anything more for the king than a one-night stand.

He sucked in a breath. It was better this way. They'd both had what they'd wanted, and it would have to be enough. Yakim needed to forget about Lucifer and focus on his job.

He didn't know if he could.

CHAPTER NINE

Lucifer was being forced to allow Berith's healer to give him a check-up. He didn't enjoy being forced into doing anything, and the only reason he'd agreed was that it had been obvious that both Berith and Yakim would feel better if they had confirmation that Lucifer wasn't hurt.

He wasn't. His bodyguard might have been good at his job, but he was nothing compared to the king of Hell. Lucifer had defended himself easily. There wasn't even a scratch on him.

He couldn't say the same for Barnum and poor Sahndra. He needed to find Bretton and tell him to take care of her body. He didn't care what happened to Barnum's body, but Sahndra had died protecting him, and that meant something. He wanted her to be honored and for her family to never have to worry about what would happen to them. He'd take care of them until every single one was gone.

"He's fine, your Highness," the healer said as he bowed to Berith.

Berith eyed Lucifer as if he didn't believe his healer. It was ridiculous. Lucifer knew that Reyni was Berith and Mel's healer, which meant that Berith trusted him with his life.

"I really am," Lucifer confirmed. "Barnum didn't touch me."

"He didn't do a good job, then," Berith said.

"I don't believe he was paid to kill me because he could do a good job, but rather because of how close he was to me."

"I should have looked into his past more," Bretton muttered.

He was sitting on one of the couches in Berith's office, looking like he wanted to drink himself to sleep. Like Lucifer had expected, he'd taken the news hard that one of the bodyguards he'd handpicked had tried to kill Lucifer. Lucifer had attempted to tell him it wasn't his fault, but from Bretton's grim expression, he didn't think Bretton believed him.

Lucifer relaxed on the couch he was sitting on. "You did look into his past."

"Not enough."

"Some people do stupid things, even when they have an impeccable past. I'm sure he was offered enough money that he felt he couldn't refuse. He had to have known it would take more than a knife to take me down, yet that's what he used. Even more, he knew how powerful I was and that there was no way he'd be able to kill me."

"That may be why he tried to surprise you," Berith said. He turned to Reyni. "Thank you. I don't believe we need you anymore, but please, go visit Mel. He said he's fine, but he was a bit shaken."

"Of course. As always, it was my pleasure, although I would appreciate it if you and your guests tried not to get yourself killed too often. I have other patients," the healer snarked.

Lucifer was impressed. Most people respected Berith but were also afraid of him and would never dare talk to him like that, yet Reyni hadn't hesitated. It sounded like he talked to Berith like that all the time, and if Lucifer hadn't known it would be impossible for him to poach the healer, he might have tried. He needed more people who told him the truth as it was instead of the version they thought he'd enjoy or want.

Luckily, it looked like Berith felt the same way. He laughed and clapped Reyni's shoulder, gently pushing him toward the door. "I get it, and we'll try our best not to get ourselves killed. Now go back to your many patients."

Reyni bowed and obeyed. Mikal, Lon's second in command, was hovering next to the door, and he quickly opened it. He hesitated, then turned to Berith, who rolled his eyes.

"Walk him back to the infirmary," he ordered.

Reyni's back stiffened. "I don't need to be walked back anywhere."

"Probably not, but I'd feel better knowing you're protected."

"I thought you'd killed every member of the society in this palace."

"I have, and don't argue my orders, please. After what happened, we all need to be reassured."

Reyni looked like he wanted to tell Berith to fuck off, but instead, he nodded stiffly and walked out the door. Mikal quickly followed him, and Berith waited until the door was closed behind them to speak.

"I swear, those two will never get their heads out of their asses. Well, Mikal has, but Reyni? It sounds impossible."

Lucifer gaped. "Are you trying to set them up?"

Berith shrugged. "Mel thinks they'd be good together, and I can't say I disagree. Besides, Mikal has a crush as big as the palace on Reyni. I'm not sure if Reyni knows it or if he's just ignoring it, but everyone's had enough of the two of them dancing around each other. Mikal looks like a lost puppy most of the time, while Reyni has been even grumpier lately. I can't have a grumpy healer."

Lucifer hadn't expected that kind of behavior from his friend, but he should have. Berith had always been a nice person, and things had changed for the better after he'd met Mel. Being with the human had softened him, and while he still stood strong against his enemies and whoever threatened to hurt him or his family, the softness was a nice addition. He didn't only want people to survive anymore. He wanted people to thrive, and he did what he could to make that happen.

Berith clapped his hands. "Anyway. Enough talking about those two since there's nothing we can do about them. You don't have any bodyguards anymore, and you need some. Yakim, you're assigned to him until he leaves."

Lucifer blinked. He hadn't understood why Berith had asked Yakim to follow them to his office, but now, he did. He'd clearly been planning this since they'd been in the hallway, and Lucifer wasn't sure what to think.

Was Berith trying to set them up like he was with Reyni and Mikal? Lucifer had no doubt Berith was worried about him now that he didn't have bodyguards and that he wanted someone he trusted to watch his back, but there had to be someone else.

"I'm not sure that's a good idea, your Highness," Yakim quickly said. "I already have enough work watching your consort."

"Well, you don't have to watch him for now. I've already talked to Mel, and he agrees to stick mostly to his classroom and our private wing. He'll be with me, Lon, Roque, and if we need anyone else, Mikal. He'll be protected."

Lucifer watched Yakim. It was clear that he wanted to continue arguing, but also that he knew Berith was his king and that he needed to accept whatever order he was given.

That made Lucifer feel a little sad. He didn't want him to be forced to stay with him if he didn't want to. He was still planning to seduce him, but forced proximity might not be the best way to do that.

But he couldn't refuse Berith's help. Berith cared about him and was trying to protect him by assigning the people he trusted the most to him. Lucifer was grateful and humbled, but also delighted. This might not be what he wanted, but Lucifer would make the most out of it.

He hadn't missed the way Yakim had put more distance between them in the hallway after Berith had declared he was happy Lucifer would be leaving soon. Lucifer was planning to go back to his palace, but only temporarily. He had every intention of coming back and moving to the area. Maybe that wasn't clear to Yakim.

Lucifer would make sure it was. He also would make sure Yakim knew how he felt about him and what he wanted from him. Lucifer had no idea what Yakim would think or feel about all of that, but he'd find out soon.

He was both elated and terrified at the thought.

Yakim couldn't continue arguing. Anyone else would have been honored to be chosen by the prince to protect the king of Hell, and Yakim was, but he was also conflicted.

Berith trusted him. He wouldn't have assigned him to Mel's protection otherwise. It had been an honor to be asked to protect the prince's consort, and this was an honor, too, but in a different way. Berith deemed Yakim good enough to protect the king of Hell, of all people, the most powerful and important demon in Hell. Everyone would know that, even if they didn't know how good Yakim was at his job.

But they wouldn't know that Yakim and Lucifer had sex in the garden on a stone bench. They wouldn't know that Yakim had no idea what was happening between them or what he should do about it.

He'd thought he wanted Lucifer to go back to his palace, but finding out that he was going to do so soon had thrown him off guard. He didn't want Lucifer to go back, but he understood the king couldn't stay much longer. Since Lucifer was leaving, Yakim should keep as much distance from him as possible, but instead, Berith was throwing them together.

How was that supposed to help? Yakim wasn't an idiot. He and everyone else at the palace knew that Berith wanted Reyni to get his head out of his ass and see that Mikal was in love with him. He thought they'd be a good couple, and he was probably right, but the situation between Yakim and Lucifer was completely different. Berith couldn't be thinking of setting them up, could he? He had to know there was no way Yakim could be with the king of Hell.

He cleared his throat. "Will I have to follow the king once he goes back to his palace?" Berith had made it sound like that would happen soon, and Yakim wanted to make sure he wasn't ordering him to follow Lucifer. As much as he liked Lucifer, he couldn't leave his life behind.

"I would never ask you to leave this place," Berith promised. "When Lucifer goes back, you'll return to Mel's side."

"I don't want to go back, anyway," Lucifer grumbled.

Yakim already knew that. Lucifer hadn't been shy about how much he hated living in his palace during family dinners and when he was surrounded by people he trusted. Yakim didn't fully understand why, and he didn't think he could unless he went there and saw the situation for himself.

That was something he was never planning on doing.

"It would probably be safer to go back," Bretton said carefully. "I know we talked about finding you a palace close by, but considering what just happened, you'll be safer back home."

Yakim could tell from Lucifer's expression he was going to be stubborn about this, and he wasn't the only one. Bretton's eyes narrowed, and he crossed his arms over his chest, glaring at his boss. That didn't stop Lucifer. Yakim was pretty sure nothing could stop him when he wanted something, and clearly, he wanted to stay in the area.

"How is that search for a new palace going?" Lucifer asked.

"I'm not saying you can never move here, although I'll continue to advise you that it's not the best idea. I won't try to stop you, but until we have a safe place for you and new bodyguards, you need to be careful. I mean no offense to Prince

Berith, and we did bring in the snake who tried to kill you, but this isn't my domain. I'd feel much better if we were back at the palace."

"Well, I wouldn't," Lucifer declared. "I understand what you're saying. You don't have your spies and the rest of your people here, and I get that. But as you just pointed out, we brought in the demon who tried to kill me. Berith had nothing to do with that. It wasn't one of his people. You might feel like we're not safe here, but I doubt I'll be any safer back at the palace. That place is a nest of vipers, and I'm sure that one of them paid my bodyguard to kill me. You want me to go back to these people? Without even knowing who was behind it?"

That seems to give Bretton pause. "I don't want anything to happen to you. You might not trust anyone at the palace, but there are several people I do trust, and they'd keep you safe."

"Not any safer than Yakim can keep me, and I'm not saying that just because I like him. Berith trusts his people. He got rid of the enemies in his palace, which means that the people who remain are loyal to him. They won't go against him and hurt me."

Yakim wasn't sure what to think about how much faith Lucifer had in him. It was humbling, but at the same time, it made him panic. What if something happened to Lucifer while Yakim was supposed to watch his back? He wasn't infallible. He did his best to protect the people he was tasked to protect, but there were times when things went wrong. He might be responsible for the death of the king of Hell, and that wasn't something he could wrap his mind around or that he wanted to consider.

"You're both welcome to stay as long as you want," Berith interjected. "My home is yours, and it's as safe as it can be, considering who you are. I can't promise no one is going to try to hurt you, but I do believe we took out everyone working against me. I understand why Bretton feels you have to go back, but I want to assure both of you that I'll protect Lucifer with my life. He's not just my king, but also my friend."

Bretton sighed. "I know. You don't have to be so formal, Berith. We're all friends here, and I know you'd never forgive yourself if anything happened to Lucifer. I just don't like not having my spies."

"Maybe you could have access to ours," Lon suggested. "As long as they know we trust you, they shouldn't have a problem with that."

"I suppose it would be better than nothing," Bretton said slowly.

It looked like Yakim was stuck. He doubted anything he could say would convince Berith to place him back with Mel, which meant he'd have to spend the next few days protecting Lucifer. He had no idea what would happen during those days, but he'd do his job and protect Lucifer to the best of his ability. He'd keep the king of Hell safe.

He wasn't sure he could do the same for his own heart.

Lucifer didn't know how Berith had managed it, but he'd done something Lucifer had never managed—convinced Bretton to do something he wasn't happy with.

Lucifer had agreed with Bretton that they needed to go back to the palace, even if it was only for however much time it took to check who was doing what there and who was trying to kill Lucifer. Lucifer didn't know how long that would take, but he didn't want to stay there for long. He'd be welcome to come back to Berith's palace once that was done, but could he really do so?

Berith would welcome him with open arms whenever he decided to return. They were friends, and that was more important than anything else they could be to each other. If trouble was following Lucifer, though, he didn't want to bring it back to Berith's door, especially with Mel living in the palace. He would never forgive himself if something happened to Berith's consort.

"I'll try to find out who's behind this, then," Bretton said. He hesitated. "And since you've already decided we're not going back, it would probably be a good idea to take a step back from all of this," he told Lucifer. "You're extremely visible. Whoever paid your bodyguard to kill you will know you're alive soon, if they don't already. They'll try to kill you again."

"What do you want me to do? Hide?" That wasn't a bad idea. Lucifer knew Yakim would protect him, but he didn't want anything to happen to him as he did so. Yakim was a very capable demon, but that didn't mean he couldn't be hurt. Lucifer wanted to protect *him*, but he doubted that saying it out loud would help.

He was sure Yakim wanted him as much as he wanted Yakim, and now that he was, he had some planning and wooing to do. He didn't have a problem leaving the problem of who was trying to kill him in Bretton and Berith's capable hands. He trusted them to find the culprit and bring them to him.

In the meantime, he'd focus on Yakim.

He probably shouldn't be planning to seduce his bodyguard, but he trusted Berith to keep him safe even when Yakim was distracted. Hiding didn't sound like such a bad idea. That way, Lucifer and Yakim would both be safe, and Lucifer would have the time and space to make Yakim see they were perfect for each other.

Their differences didn't matter, not in the way Yakim thought. From where Lucifer stood, it looked like their differences meant they'd work together better than if they were similar. Even if that wasn't true, Yakim would be able to protect himself much better than any other consort ever could.

But Lucifer wasn't planning to bring up the consort thing anytime soon. It was a sure way to send Yakim into hiding, and that was the last thing Lucifer wanted.

"You mentioned wanting to visit the human realm," Berith said.

Lucifer had no idea how Berith could remember that, but he nodded. "I go there regularly to pick up a few things I particularly enjoy." Like his tea and good chocolate. He'd kill for good chocolate.

"Why don't you go now? It would keep you out of reach of the demons trying to kill you. Yakim can go with you and protect you, but unless these people find out where you are and send someone after you, you'll be safer than you can be anywhere in Hell."

Lucifer thought it was a good idea, but he turned to Bretton to check. He appeared pensive, but eventually, he nodded.

"It *is* a good idea," Bretton confirmed. "Even if someone tries to kill Lucifer again, it will be easier to defend him with so few demons around. The distance will take him away from the society until we can make sure they won't hurt him."

"I agree," Lucifer said before turning to Yakim.

Yakim's expression was enough to tell Lucifer he wasn't okay with this. Was he going to try to convince Berith to change his mind? Lucifer doubted he would normally, but the situation was anything but normal.

"My prince, I'm not sure I can go to the human realm," Yakim said slowly.

"I understand it might be difficult for you, but I truly believe this is the best thing we can do to protect Lucifer," Berith said. "I doubt your father will find you, even if he knows you're there."

Lucifer remembered that Yakim had a human father. It made him curious, but it didn't look like Yakim wanted to see the man. Lucifer didn't know nearly enough about Yakim's parentage and his past, and that was a problem he needed to fix. The time he and Yakim would spend together would help with that.

"And Mel has been saying he wants to visit his family and spend a little time in the human realm," Berith continued. "We could send the four of you."

"I don't know if that's a good idea," Yakim said. "If someone attacks Lucifer, Mel might end up in the middle of it."

"I trust you and Roque to keep him and Lucifer safe. In the human realm, no one will know who you are. As long as you don't make a spectacle of yourself, you'll be safe."

Lucifer hoped he was right. It was true that when he went to the human realm, people noticed him a lot less than they did here in Hell, even with his two bodyguards following him. That was one of the reasons he enjoyed spending time there. Here, he was the king, but in the human realm, he was just another demon. He was anonymous, and it made him feel normal. He liked the human world, and he was excited to show Yakim as much of it as he could.

If Yakim would let him.

Yakim didn't want to go to the human realm. He understood that the chances that he'd see his father were close to zero—he knew the man's name and the city he lived in, but that was it. He was sure that if he tried, he could find him, but he wasn't ashamed to admit to himself that he was scared.

His mother had never rejected him, but she'd also only done the bare minimum. All his life, Yakim had thought it was all she could give him. He'd believed demons didn't love, not even their children. He knew that wasn't true now. He'd seen demons love others, like Berith. Berith loved Mel more than life itself, and he'd sacrifice anything for him, something Yakim's mother would never even have thought of doing.

Yakim's father was an unknown entity. Yakim only knew that he was human. Maybe he was a nice human like Mel, or maybe he was horrible, and that was why his mother had left. It was impossible to find out without getting her to talk about it, and Yakim was never going back there.

But this trip wasn't about his father. It was about keeping Lucifer safe, and right now, that was *Yakim's* job. Berith's order was to take Lucifer to the human realm and protect him, and that was what Yakim would do.

Yakim bowed to his prince. "Of course."

Berith looked at him as if he hadn't expected him to give in so easily. Sometimes, it was hard to work for him because their boundaries weren't fixed. Yakim was a guard, so Berith was his boss and ordered him around, but at the same time, Yakim had spent so much time with the prince and his family that he felt like he was almost part of it. When he wasn't working, and even sometimes when he was, Berith treated him like they were friends. Friends wouldn't order each other around, but Berith had to order Yakim to do this.

Maybe he didn't know that Yakim would do what he wanted even if he didn't use his authority. It didn't matter to him that Berith was a prince. He was a friend, and if he believed Yakim should do this, then Yakim would do it.

"I'm sure Mel will be happy," Berith said.

Yakim nodded curtly. "I'll protect him and Lucifer with my life."

"I know you will. And I wouldn't worry too much about your father if I were you. I doubt he can find you if you don't contact him." Berith hesitated. "Unless that's something you'd like to do?"

Yakim shook his head instantly. He didn't give himself time to think about it because this trip wasn't about him. He couldn't afford to be distracted, especially not by his father.

That didn't mean he didn't wish he could see him. He

wanted to know more about the man, to find out what had happened and why his mother had brought him back to Hell. He couldn't help but wonder if his father had been okay with it or if he'd tried to stop her. Had he been looking for him for the past decades?

Feelings were complicated, and Yakim didn't have time to deal with them.

"I'm not planning to try to find him," he promised.

"As long as you know that you can if you wish. You're going there to protect Lucifer, but I don't expect you to work twenty-four-seven. You've never been to the human realm as an adult, and while you can always travel there, this might be your only opportunity to find him."

"But this trip isn't the right moment to find him. I can go whenever I want. I could have gone many times in the past, but I haven't. I'll be fine." Yakim hadn't gone because he'd been terrified, but Berith didn't need to know that.

"All right. We'll start organizing everything, and while the four of you are in the human realm, we'll look into who might have paid Lucifer's bodyguard to kill him."

Yakim wanted to look at the king, but he didn't dare. He and Lucifer were going to spend a lot of time together in the human realm. Even with Roque and Mel there, they were bound to be alone many times, and Yakim didn't know how he'd deal with that.

Was there anything between them beyond what had happened in the garden? Would something start while they were in the human realm? That wasn't the reason they were going there, but Yakim wasn't an idiot. There had been something growing between them since the first time they'd seen each other, and the only reason they weren't together was that Yakim had been avoiding Lucifer and telling himself that the king was leaving and that it meant there was no future between them. He still wasn't convinced about that , but if there was one thing he knew about Lucifer, it was that the king was used to getting what he wanted. He would never force Yakim into anything, but he wouldn't have to. Yakim wanted him more than he'd ever wanted anyone else.

And they were going to be stuck in the human realm for who knew how long.

This was going to be a disaster, wasn't it?

CHAPTER TEN

Yakim was nervous. He was sure he was hiding it well and that no one around him could tell, but he couldn't help feeling that way. He'd been in the human realm before, but he'd been a baby. He didn't remember anything about it, even though he'd been born there.

What would it be like? How would people behave when they saw him? Would they be able to tell that he was part human like them?

Yakim had heard from other demons who visited the human realm that demons weren't accepted there. They were kept apart from humans, and, most of the time they were treated like they were little more than animals or monsters. It was one of the reasons Yakim hadn't gone. He'd wanted to find his father, but he'd been terrified about his father's reaction. What if he didn't want to get to know Yakim? What if he was horrified at the thought that he'd fathered a half-demon?

Besides, Yakim had work to do.

He glanced sideways at Lucifer, who was talking to Berith. Roque was saying goodbye to his latest conquest while Mel was digging in his bag. For now, they were safe. They were in the portal room, which was the most protected area in the palace. Only Berith and a few trusted guards had access to it, so Lucifer and Mel were as safe as they would ever be.

Yakim didn't know what to expect from this trip. He'd be working, and that was fine with him, but how would he feel being so close to his father? He'd always wondered what the man was like, and this might be his only chance to find out.

Yet, he wouldn't allow himself to do so. He didn't think he

could. He might find out that his father had been looking for him the entire time or that he'd never wanted him to begin with. Yakim's heart would be broken, and it might make working impossible for him. He couldn't afford for that to happen. He needed to do his job and keep Lucifer and Mel safe, which meant focusing on them, not on himself and his hurt feelings.

It was better not to allow himself the distraction. It didn't make him feel great, but that was okay. He didn't have to feel great about any of this. He just had to do his job.

"Are you all right?" Mel asked, moving closer.

Yakim nodded at him. From Mel's expression, he knew he wasn't fooling the prince's consort. Maybe if he agreed that he was fine whenever someone asked him, they'd eventually believe him.

"He'll be fine," Mel said.

Yakim wondered who he was talking about. Yakim's father? No, that was impossible. "Who will be fine?"

"Lucifer. We're going to the human realm because he was attacked, but he defended himself and kicked ass. He'll be fine, even if something happens while we're in the human realm."

Yakim hadn't realized that Mel believed he was anxious because of Lucifer. Maybe he didn't know about Yakim's father. Maybe he did know but didn't understand why it would make him nervous.

"I know he can defend himself," Yakim said. "I'm pretty much useless to him as a bodyguard, but that won't stop me from protecting him. I doubt we'll have any kind of trouble, though. No one in the human realm will know who he is, and even if the people after him find out he's there, they'll have a hard time sending someone after him."

Because the portals from Hell to the human realm were few and far between. Most of the time, demons had to travel a long way to get to one, which meant that they needed to be fully convinced of what they were doing. Only a few people could open portals when and where they wanted, and they were the strongest and more powerful demons in Hell, like Lucifer and Berith. Everyone else used existing portals, so unless the people at the head of the society were as strong as a prince of Hell, they'd have to do the same. Berith and Lucifer were counting on the society not being that powerful, and Yakim hoped they weren't wrong.

Mel cocked his head. "You want to talk about the reason you're worried? Berith told me a few things, but I think he didn't want to talk too much about it in case you weren't okay with me knowing."

Yakim didn't care who knew that his father was human. He did care about how many people realized how nervous he was over that, but Mel wasn't one of those people. He was a good man, and he'd never use it against him. Yakim didn't want to talk about his father, but Mel was a friend, and he'd be hurt if Yakim brushed him off. Yakim didn't want him to be.

"You already know my father is human," he said.

Mel nodded quickly. "I would never have guessed, if that's what you're worried about."

"It's not. I'm worried because I don't know anything about him. I realize I probably won't see him while we're in the human realm, but I don't know much about him. My mother took me back to Hell when I was a baby, so I was born in the human realm. I have no idea how my father felt about that or about me leaving. I don't even know if he cared."

"I'm sure he did. I realize it's almost impossible for a human to move to Hell, but maybe they tried and couldn't make it work."

Yakim doubted that his mother had cared enough. His father couldn't survive in Hell, so his mother should have stayed in the human realm. She probably would have if she'd cared about him.

But she hadn't. She'd brought Yakim back and refused to tell him anything about his father beyond his name and the city he lived in. Even those details had only been revealed when she'd been drunk one night.

He shook his head. "I don't know what happened, and I might never find out. Either way, we're not going to the human realm to find my father, so I shouldn't worry about it."

"Maybe you shouldn't, but it doesn't mean you won't be. You can't control your emotions. Sometimes, they're big and uncomfortable, but locking them away and ignoring them is the worst thing you can do."

Yakim arched a brow. "You realize I'm not one of your children, right?"

Mel's cheeks flushed. "I know. But you're my friend, and I want to help you. What do you want?"

"I don't know."

That was the truth. Part of Yakim was desperate to meet his father, but another part kept telling himself that he was fine even without knowing anything about the man. Maybe if Yakim could be sure that his father would welcome him with open arms, he'd want to meet him. He couldn't be sure, though, and he was scared.

"That's all right. You don't have to know right now. Besides, we'll be in the human realm for at least a week, maybe more. You'll have all the time in the world to think about what you want."

"Are you sure you want to stay away from Berith for that long?"

Mel sighed. "I'll miss him, but that will only make my return sweeter, don't you think? I'm looking forward to spending time in the human realm and with my family. It would be great if Berith could be with me, but I understand he needs to stay, and that's all right. We're in love but not attached at the hip."

Yakim almost rolled his eyes. "All right. I'll protect you with my life."

"I hope you won't have to sacrifice yourself for me."

Yakim hoped the same, but he would if it was necessary, and they both knew it.

Lucifer looked around one last time. Everyone was here and ready, and if he didn't open the portal soon, Mel would start crying again, and Berith would probably change his mind about letting him go to the human realm. Those two were deeply in love, but Lucifer suspected it would do both of them good to be away from each other for a little bit.

In Hell, Mel had a limited number of people he was close to. That meant he and Berith spent a lot of time together, maybe too much. Mel depended on Berith a lot, and while Lucifer would never say anything about it, he believed it would do Mel good to be a bit more independent. In the human realm, he wouldn't have to worry about being attacked because of who he was to Berith. He had a bodyguard, even though, from what Lucifer had seen, Roque was more like a friend to Mel than anything else. They were almost family, and hopefully, it would help Mel relax. He might be happy in Hell by Berith's side, but it didn't mean he didn't miss anything from the human realm.

"Ready?" Lucifer asked.

The three who would come with him nodded. Lucifer looked at Berith, who did the same, even though he looked like he wanted to snatch Mel away and take him back to their room. Lucifer grinned at him and didn't give him time to do so. He raised a hand, focused on one of his apartments in the human realm, and opened the portal.

He had several places in the human realm, but he had his favorites. This apartment was one of those, but it wasn't the only reason he'd chosen it. He and Berith had talked last night as they got everything together for the trip, and Berith had mentioned that this was where Yakim's father used to live.

Their information on the human was as old as Yakim, so he might have moved or died or who knew what else. If he was still alive and in the city, though, Lucifer could find him. Lucifer wouldn't push Yakim to do anything he didn't feel ready for, but maybe finding his father would do him good — as long as the human was one of the good ones, anyway. If he was cruel or didn't care about Yakim, Lucifer would make sure he paid for that. He wouldn't be as thorough as he might have been with a demon, but that didn't mean he couldn't hand out punishment.

"I'll see you soon," he heard Berith promise.

He didn't have to turn to know that Berith and Mel were hugging again. He trusted Roque and Yakim to drag Mel to the portal if needed, so he stepped forward, ready to walk through the portal.

Yakim's hand shot out. "I'll go first."

"I opened the portal directly in my apartment. There's nothing dangerous there."

Yakim's expression was serious. "I'll be the judge of that. I'm going first."

Lucifer huffed but gestured at Yakim to go on, even though he felt it wasn't necessary. His apartment was safe, and he'd made sure no one but the people he wanted there could enter, even when he wasn't present. Still, if it helped Yakim feel better, Lucifer didn't have a problem with him exploring the place before they went.

Thankfully, the apartment wasn't large. It was luxurious because Lucifer could afford it and enjoyed luxury, but it only had three bedrooms, an office, a kitchen, and a living area.

He'd never had guests there, and he hadn't expected to have them, but he'd fallen in love with the place as soon as he'd seen it, so he'd bought it even though it was too big for him. He was glad he had now. There wouldn't have been enough room if he'd chosen a smaller place. Someone would have to share as it was, although he'd heard the two bodyguards talking and was pretty sure at least one of them would be awake at night. They'd probably take turns. Lucifer wanted to tell them it wasn't necessary, but he realized this was their job and he needed to allow them to do it.

He turned to Mel and Berith. Berith caught his gaze, and Lucifer arched a brow, tilting his chin toward Mel. Berith looked like he might growl at him for trying to take away his consort, but he gave Mel a gentle push instead.

"You should go. Your family is expecting you, and you'll want to change and get your bearings before heading there."

Mel was a bit teary-eyed, but he nodded and grabbed two of his bags. Roque made a wounded sound and darted forward, but Mel raised his chin high and refused to let him take them from him. "I'm not weak. I can carry two bags."

"I never said you were weak."

"But you behave like I am. Take the other bags, and let's go."

The consort had given his orders, and Roque followed them.

Lucifer glanced at Berith one last time and nodded. "He'll be safe. I'll make sure of it."

"I know. Stay safe, too, though."

"You won't get rid of me that easily. I'll be back soon, and you'll complain I wasn't gone long enough."

"Never."

Lucifer chuckled, grabbed his bags, and followed Mel through the portal.

It closed behind him, and like always when he first arrived

in the human realm, he took a moment to allow his eyes to adapt to the light. It was much brighter here and hurt a little, but the sensation vanished quickly.

He looked around. Mel and Roque were standing in the middle of the room, talking to each other. There were no signs of Yakim, but the bags he'd been carrying had been left next to the couch. If Lucifer focused, he could hear him walking around the apartment. He was making sure they were safe, even though it was unnecessary.

Lucifer smiled at Mel. "If you'll allow me to show you to the guest room," he offered.

"I will, but can you please not be so formal?"

Lucifer laughed. "Of course. How about while we're in the human realm, we're just Lucifer and Mel?"

"I don't think you can ever be just Lucifer, but that's fine with me."

"Wait until Yakim is back," Roque said.

Lucifer almost rolled his eyes. "Do you really think there's anything I can't defend Mel from? Especially in the human realm?"

Roque's spine stiffened as if he realized he'd just told Lucifer he couldn't protect himself and Mel. "Of course not, your Highness. I apologize."

"Don't worry about it. I'll protect Mel with my life. There really is nothing to worry about, though. He's safe here, as am I." The only thing Lucifer risked was indigestion from eating too much chocolate, but he needed to buy it first.

Lucifer took the bags from Mel, glad when Mel didn't try to stop him like he had Roque, and gently guided the human deeper into the apartment. He'd opened the portal in the living room, so he showed Mel the rooms as they walked. It didn't take long to explain where everything was in the kitchen and that Mel would have his own private bathroom attached to his bedroom.

"I need to change," Mel said as he looked around the guest room. "I love these clothes when I'm in Hell, but here, they feel out of place, even though there's no one to see me."

He wore the usual flowy clothing in Hell because of the heat. It made sense that it made him feel exposed, especially since it was nowhere near as hot here as it was in Hell.

Lucifer lightly bowed at him. "I'll give you some space, then. You know where to find everything."

"I do. Thank you."

"It's my pleasure to have you here with me."

It really was. Usually, Lucifer came to the human realm with only a few bodyguards but no one he considered a friend. He and Mel had only recently met, but he felt close to the human, and he loved how Mel had transformed Berith. If there was anything he could do for Mel, he'd do it.

"One last thing," Mel said before Lucifer could leave.

"Do you need anything else?"

"No, but I'd like to find Yakim's father. I asked Berith about him, so I have a few details, but I wouldn't know where to start looking."

"Does Yakim want you to find him?"

Mel's sheepish expression was enough to tell Lucifer the answer. "I don't think so, but even if we do find him, it's not like he has to see him. There's no way to know if we'll be able to locate the man, but I want Yakim to have the opportunity to meet him if he wants to. Will you just look into it for me? Don't tell Yakim anything, but try to find him. We can go from there."

Lucifer didn't want to do anything that would cause Yakim to be angry at him, but Mel was right. Even if he did find Yakim's father, he wouldn't force him to visit him. He'd be able to give him an address and a name, and Yakim could do whatever he wanted with it.

Maybe it wasn't such a bad idea after all.

CHAPTER ELEVEN

One of the things Lucifer enjoyed the most when he spent time in the human realm was that he didn't owe anyone anything. He didn't have a schedule, anything pressing to do, people to meet, or anything like that. It was peaceful when Bretton wasn't running after him, telling him where and when to go.

After they'd settled in yesterday, Lucifer had stayed in the apartment. Mel had visited with his family for a few hours, then spent the rest of the afternoon poking around the apartment, seemingly delighted with how many books Lucifer had accumulated and happy to watch TV and relax. He looked at peace on Lucifer's couch, and Lucifer made a mental note to tell Berith to bring his human to the human realm more often. He didn't always have to go with him if that was what worried him, but it would be nice for the two of them to be allowed to relax without having to think about the job.

But that was yesterday, and Lucifer was ready to get busy. He'd already started looking into Yakim's father. While he agreed with Mel that Yakim didn't have to do anything with the information he might find, he still felt uncomfortable doing this without him knowing. Mel would be disappointed, but Lucifer had decided he needed to talk to Yakim. Maybe talking about his father would help him. If anything, it would help Lucifer understand how he felt about finding him.

The two bodyguards had relaxed, since they hadn't left the apartment yet today. They were still being careful, but the doors were locked, and Lucifer had ensured that no one could get to the apartment without him knowing. He'd warded the area in front of his door, along with the two entrances to the building. He'd know if a demon attempted to sneak in.

He found Yakim relaxing on the wide terrace. He was sitting at the table by the open door, reading a book, but he looked up as soon as he heard Lucifer. He quickly dropped the book to the table and scrambled to get to his feet, but Lucifer shook his head and gestured at him to stay where he was.

"I'm just going to sit with you," he said.

"Can I get you anything, your Highness?"

Lucifer scowled. "You can stop calling me *your Highness*, to begin with. I thought we were past that." He leaned closer and lowered his voice so that only Yakim could hear him. "Especially after what happened in the garden."

Yakim looked away, but thankfully, he didn't argue. Lucifer wasn't sure he'd call him by his name, but he'd tried.

"I'm sorry to bother you," he began.

"You're not bothering me."

"I can see that I am, since you were reading. And don't bother telling me that you're here to serve me or something just as stupid."

Yakim arched a brow. "Why did you allow me to come if not to serve you? Do you want in my bed so badly?"

For a second, Lucifer was stunned by Yakim's answer. He would never have expected him to say something like that.

He burst out laughing. "I won't deny that I do want in your bed quite badly, but no. I wanted you here for your company, which I quite enjoy."

Yakim looked like he didn't believe it, but he didn't argue. He waited for Lucifer to say what he was here to say, but Lucifer was finding it difficult. He didn't want to hurt Yakim, and he suspected that knowing he was looking into his father would do just that. Lucifer could stop, but something told him that Yakim might need this kind of closure. Even if he found out his father was an asshole, at least he'd know.

Lucifer hated his family, but he knew how they were and not to expect anything from them. He couldn't imagine what it would be like to wonder about his father all of his life. If anything he could do helped Yakim get peace of mind, he wanted to do it.

Lucifer thrummed his fingertips on top of the table. "Mel talked to me about your father yesterday," he started.

Yakim's entire body tensed. Lucifer waited for him to tell him to fuck off, but he didn't. It was probably only because of who Lucifer was, and while Lucifer would usually dislike that, right now, he'd take it as a win. It meant Yakim would listen to him, and that was all he wanted.

"Mel asked me to find him. Before you get angry at him, he told me that he wouldn't tell you anything about the man unless you wanted to know, but he thought it would be a good thing to at least know where he is."

"Why are you telling me that if Mel didn't want me to know?"

"Because I dislike the thought of doing this behind your back. I know we haven't promised anything to each other, but what happened in the garden meant something. You're important to me, and I never want to do anything that would hurt you."

Yakim was silent for a moment. He looked out at the city beyond the terrace, and Lucifer did the same. The view was one of the reasons he'd bought the apartment, and he always spent a lot of time on the terrace when he visited. Sometimes, he wondered if it would be selfish to move here and never go back to Hell.

It would be. So many demons would get hurt if he did that.

"I'm not hurt," Yakim eventually said. "Confused, mostly. I don't understand why this is so important to you and Mel."

Lucifer leaned back in his chair. "Well, we obviously care

about you. I don't know about Mel, but I can see that you're always a little lost."

"I'm not," Yakim said quickly.

"Maybe lost isn't the right word. But I was thinking that I know my father. I've known him all my life, so I'm very much aware of the fact that he's a cruel asshole who shouldn't be in charge of Hell. I know him and my sister. I don't like them, but they're my family, and it means I know where I come from. I strive to be different from them, which is one reason I'm so good at being king. Not that I'm saying you're not good at being a bodyguard, because you are. I just believe that it would help you to know who your father is and, more importantly, why he's not in your life."

"I already know why he's not in my life. He can't come to Hell. He's human."

"But you don't know if he would come if he could."

"My mother never told me how he reacted when she decided to take me back. Actually, I don't even know if he's aware I exist. As far as I know, she could have had me without telling him she was pregnant."

"And you've wanted to know most of your life, haven't you?"

"I want to know where I come from. I'm aware that it might go badly and that maybe he never wanted me, and if that's what happened, I'll deal with it. But you're right. I want to know where I come from. I like my present, but I don't know my past, and it feels like there's something missing."

"So you want me to continue looking for him?"

There was a moment of silence before Yakim answered. "If you can, I want you to find him."

Yakim couldn't believe those words had come out of his mouth. He shouldn't have told Lucifer that he wanted him to look for his father, but he'd been curious about the man since he was old enough to understand what a father was, and his mother's refusal to tell him anything about him hadn't helped. Yakim yearned to find out what had happened between them and what kind of person his father was, and this might be the only opportunity he had to do so.

He didn't know if he'd ever come back to the human realm. He hadn't seen much of it because he and Lucifer had stayed in the apartment since they'd arrived yesterday, but from what he'd observed from the windows, it didn't look too bad. The majority of the people he'd watched were human, but he'd seen a few demons here and there, and they'd been fine. No one had tried to hurt them, and while it had been clear that some of the humans didn't like them, it wasn't worse than what demons had to deal with in Hell.

Neither Hell nor the human world were great, which probably meant they were more similar than anyone expected.

"You're sure?" Lucifer asked.

He wasn't surprised that Lucifer wanted confirmation. Yakim had refused to let anyone help him with his father his entire life. Berith had offered to find him a few times, but Yakim had always said no. It wouldn't have changed anything for him since he'd been in Hell and had no plans on leaving.

He *had* left. He was in the same realm as his father for the first time since he was a baby. "I'm sure," he confirmed. "I don't expect anything from him but the worse, so I won't be surprised if he wants nothing to do with me." His mother barely wanted anything to do with him, so it wasn't like Yakim wasn't used to it. If neither of his parents wanted him, that was fine with him. He didn't need them because he had his friends.

"All right then," Lucifer said slowly.

"It sounds like you're trying to change my mind. I thought you *wanted* me to talk to my father?"

"I wouldn't say that. I do believe it would do you good, but I won't force you, and I don't want you to be hurt. If you believe this is a bad idea, you won't have to use the information I find."

"Stop worrying so much. I've already thought about this, and I wouldn't be saying yes if I wasn't sure. If I decide to meet him, I won't hold you responsible for anything that happens."

Maybe that was why Lucifer was worried. Maybe he wanted what was happening between them to have time and space to bloom, but that wouldn't happen if Yakim got angry because his father didn't want to see him.

Yakim was done resisting this. He probably shouldn't give in, and there was no way to know how things would go once they went back to Hell, but he was tired. He wanted Lucifer, and Lucifer wanted him. Did anything else matter?

Probably, but that wouldn't stop him anymore.

He got up and moved around the table. Lucifer started doing the same, pushing his chair away from the table and turning it sideways, but Yakim reached him before he could get up. He put a hand on Lucifer's shoulder, pushed him back into the chair, and climbed into his lap.

Lucifer's hands landed on Yakim's hips as if he wanted to hold him there. He smiled, and they looked at each other in the eyes.

"I remember the last time we were in a similar position," Lucifer murmured.

"It was the other way around. You were in my lap." Yakim hooked his arms around Lucifer's shoulders. It felt so damn good to be close to him again after he'd done his best to stay away.

There was no resisting this, was there? Yakim had hoped he'd be strong enough, but it was clear every time they touched that it wasn't meant to be. He wanted Lucifer too much, and since Lucifer wanted him back, there was no way out.

Yakim didn't want one.

"We did things we shouldn't have done in a garden," Lucifer whispered as he leaned forward and pressed a kiss to Yakim's neck.

They'd been exposed in the garden, and they still were. Roque and Mel could walk in on them at any moment. The difference was that they knew there was something between Yakim and Lucifer. They wouldn't be surprised, and they wouldn't start gossiping. Maybe that was what gave Yakim the courage to lean toward Lucifer and kiss him on the lips. Whatever it was, it didn't make a difference. He wanted Lucifer, and he had him.

Even though it wasn't much yet, what they had felt important and precious. Resisting it hadn't worked, and it felt like the worst idea now. It was clear Lucifer cared about him. He was giving him the thing he'd wanted the most in the world. He would find his father, and maybe, if Yakim was lucky, he'd finally get answers to his many questions about his birth and early childhood. Even if he never got those answers, Lucifer had done this for him because he wanted him to be happy and to have everything he wished for.

Right now, the only thing Yakim wished for was Lucifer.

It felt good to be in his arms and kiss him. Lucifer cradled Yakim as if he were precious, and that wasn't something Yakim was used to.

But if they were going to work, he'd have to get used to it. It would be odd but not unpleasant, and for the first time since he and Lucifer had met during the party, Yakim allowed himself to relax and accept that whatever happened next, they'd face it together.

The attraction between them was strong and not anything Yakim had ever felt before, and Lucifer was the most wonderful man. They could have so much more, and Yakim was finally ready to find out what that more was. He was done resisting.

Even though it meant his life would change more than he could ever have expected.

CHAPTER TWELVE

Lucifer smiled at the lady behind the counter and accepted the bag she held out to him. "Thank you so very much," he said with a light bow.

Her cheeks flushed, and she leaned closer, only to stop and eye Yakim.

Lucifer might appear human, but it was very obvious that Yakim wasn't. Even though his father was human, his horns, pointed ears, long fingers tipped with claws, white eyes, and patchy skin made his demon heritage obvious. The woman was wary of him and had been since they'd walked into the shop, but Yakim had been stoic and acted like he hadn't noticed it. He'd kept his focus on Lucifer and his safety.

It didn't feel right. Lucifer had never cared about how his bodyguards were treated when he was in the human realm. He hadn't thought much about it, but now, he couldn't avoid doing so because Yakim wasn't just his bodyguard. Lucifer wanted him to experience the human world. He wanted him to taste the chocolate he'd just bought, watch a movie, and do a dozen other things. The problem was that the humans would make it difficult. They kept staring at Yakim, and it wouldn't get better.

Lucifer might feel like an outsider in Hell because he looked human, but here, it was Yakim who had to feel this way, and Lucifer disliked it. He wanted to show Yakim only the best of the human world, but he couldn't.

"I'm ready to go," Lucifer said, turning to Yakim.

He held the gaze of the woman behind the counter and

took Yakim's hand.

Yakim's eyes widened, and for a moment, Lucifer thought he'd step away. Instead, he squeezed Lucifer's fingers and pulled him outside without saying a word. Lucifer didn't look back to see how the woman reacted. He didn't care. He just wanted her to know that no matter what Yakim looked like, he was a good man.

Besides, Yakim was beautiful. His wide eyes glowed, his horns were polished, and his pointed ears were adorable. Lucifer liked every part of him and wouldn't change anything even if he could.

"That wasn't necessary," Yakim murmured as they left the store.

"What wasn't necessary was for her to stare at you the way she did," Lucifer grumbled.

"I look different. I'm not surprised she looked at me like that. She also won't be the last to do so, so maybe you should make peace with it. I don't care and don't want you to, either."

Lucifer sighed. Yakim was right. He shouldn't care about how a human woman they'd never see again looked at Yakim. "I just don't want you to regret coming here," he explained.

Yakim was still holding his hand, and he squeezed. "I don't think I could. I'm enjoying myself."

"Even with the way everyone looks at you?"

Yakim shrugged. "Everyone always looks at me, even when I'm at the palace."

"But there, they look at you because of who you are."

"I don't think it's that different. I mean, look around. I'm the tallest person on the street right now. It makes sense that the humans are looking at me, and I think they would even if I were human like them."

"I suppose you're right." As long as they didn't do or say anything bad, Lucifer supposed he should take a step back. Yakim didn't need him to protect him. He could do so himself and *would* do so if he needed to. Besides, he was here to protect Lucifer, not the other way around. They could have fun even with every single human they crossed paths watching them.

Lucifer would make sure they did.

"We should get you new clothing," he said, having decided to spoil Yakim.

Yakim appeared alarmed at the suggestion. "I don't need more clothes."

"I like what you're wearing, but maybe you could try human fashion."

Yakim looked down at himself. He was wearing his usual bodyguard uniform of long pants and a light shirt. It didn't look too much out of place in the human realm, but it also clearly didn't belong. Dressing Yakim in human clothing wouldn't change the way the humans looked at him, but Lucifer couldn't help but wonder what he would look like in a suit, with a well-fitted shirt and a tie. Would he want to roll up the sleeves of his shirt? Lucifer was a sucker for rolled-up sleeves.

"Is it necessary?" Yakim asked.

"Not necessary, but I'd really enjoy looking at you in those clothes. We don't have to buy anything if you don't want it."

"It's just that I'm not sure what I'll do with those clothes once I go back to Hell. I understand my clothing doesn't fit here, but I don't think dressing me in human clothes will change that."

"I wasn't trying to change the way you look."

Yakim arched a brow. "Isn't that kind of the point?"

"Okay, so maybe it was kind of the point, but I wasn't doing it so you could try to hide that you're a demon. You're right, and there's no hiding that. Even more importantly, you *shouldn't* have to hide it, and I don't expect you to. I want you to experience the human world and give you the best of everything."

"You already do," Yakim murmured.

He had the ability to fluster Lucifer with just a few words. Lucifer was always surprised when that happened, but he liked it.

He wasn't usually surprised by the people he slept with, except in the worst ways. They always wanted something from him, and most would have jumped on Lucifer's offer. Even worse, they would have *demanded* he buy them new clothes, jewelry, and everything they could think of. They'd have wanted Lucifer to spoil them, and he would have hated it.

But he *wanted* to spoil Yakim, and Yakim was one who hated it. The situation was almost funny, and if Lucifer needed any more proof that Yakim was the right demon for him, he had it. Yakim didn't expect anything from him and didn't *want* anything but Lucifer's attention and affection. That meant he was the perfect partner and maybe even the perfect consort.

But that wasn't something Lucifer wanted to think about right now. Instead, he wanted to think about finding a way to convince Yakim to go along with what he wanted. They couldn't go back to Hell, and they hadn't found Yakim's father yet. They didn't have anything to do, but that would probably change soon. Once they returned to Hell, they wouldn't have nearly as much time together, so Lucifer wanted to make the most out of their time in the human realm.

He didn't want to push Yakim because, as the past had shown, Yakim ran when he was pushed. Maybe Lucifer just needed to be honest and tell Yakim what he wanted and thought.

Or maybe he just needed to love Yakim. It shouldn't be too hard, since he was already in love with him.

Yakim loved Lucifer's generosity, but that didn't mean the situation didn't make him uncomfortable.

It wasn't like Lucifer was trying to buy his affection or anything like that. It didn't feel that way, and knowing Lucifer, he'd never do that. Maybe it was just that he was so used to everyone wanting something from him that it was instinct to offer first, or maybe he truly just wanted to spoil Yakim. Whatever the reason behind his behavior, it was clear it was important to him.

Yakim didn't need new clothes or anything expensive. He didn't need anything at all. Yet he'd allow Lucifer to buy him what he wanted because it put a smile on Lucifer's face, and Yakim couldn't get enough of those smiles.

He sighed. "Fine. Buy me new clothes."

The way Lucifer's expression brightened was enough to tell Yakim he'd made the right choice. He doubted he'd wear those clothes once he went back to Hell, but maybe it wasn't a bad idea for him to look a bit more human when he met his father.

He didn't know if Lucifer would be able to find him, but he had faith in the king. If there was anyone who could find his father, it would be Lucifer, which meant Yakim needed to be ready. He already knew that if Lucifer found his father, he wanted to visit him. He was ready to take whatever his father threw at him and fully expected the human not to be happy to see him. Yakim needed closure, though, and it felt like this would give it to him. Once he'd met his father, he could finally be at peace and stop asking himself questions he would never get the answer to. He'd know, and that was what felt important to him right now.

He allowed Lucifer to drag him down the street. Clearly, he knew where he was going, which wasn't a surprise considering how he dressed. His clothes had to come from the human realm, and while Yakim doubted they would fit him as well as they did Lucifer, he suspected it would make him feel like he and Lucifer matched more than they did now. The way he dressed wouldn't change the fact that he was only a bodyguard, but they would look like they fit together, and Yakim wanted that, even if it was only in the human realm.

The two of them were in a bubble where they didn't have to worry about anything but themselves. Yakim had to keep Lucifer safe, but he didn't have to worry about what would happen once they went back to Hell. Would Lucifer return to his palace? He'd been talking about finding a place closer to Berith, and Yakim was excited, but it still meant he wouldn't see Lucifer every day. He'd gotten used to it, especially since they'd arrived in the human realm. Thinking about Lucifer so far away made him sad, but what was the alternative? Moving into Lucifer's new palace with him?

Yakim couldn't imagine what that would be like. Maybe he could become Lucifer's bodyguard, although he wasn't sure Bretton would be happy with that. He'd probably say that Yakim couldn't focus enough to protect Lucifer, and he wouldn't be wrong. It was too easy to get distracted by Lucifer. At the same time, though, no one wanted to keep Lucifer safe more than Yakim. If he thought about Lucifer getting hurt, he wanted to scream, and he'd do anything to ensure that didn't happen.

He didn't have any answers when it came to this, either.

"This is my favorite store when it comes to suits and everyday clothing," Lucifer said excitedly as he pushed open the door of one of the shops lining the street.

It wasn't hard to believe. Everything inside the shop screamed luxury and elegance, just like Lucifer. Yakim had no idea what he'd look like once Lucifer was done with him, but he trusted the king.

He still did when, an hour later, they left the store. Yakim was already wearing some of the clothing Lucifer had bought for him, and he had to admit it made him look like a different person. The dress pants and shirt, along with the jacket, were comfortable enough for him to move and be able to protect Lucifer, but it made him look like just maybe, he belonged by Lucifer's side.

"You're so incredibly handsome," Lucifer gushed.

Yakim wanted to roll his eyes, but Lucifer wasn't lying. He didn't usually look at himself in the mirror and think he was handsome or ugly, but he *felt* handsome. Nothing he could do would make him look human, but he didn't *want* to look human.

Thankfully, Lucifer had had enough of his shopping session, so they headed back to the apartment. Once they were inside, Yakim allowed himself to relax because he knew Lucifer was safe. He didn't expect anything to happen there.

He certainly didn't expect the loud whistle when he stepped into the living room.

He looked around, frowning, then scowling when he found Roque staring at him from the couch. Roque whistled again, and Yakim wondered if he'd ruin his new clothes if he punched his friend.

"What happened to you?" Roque asked, getting up from the couch and coming closer.

Lucifer gently touched Yakim's back. "I'm going to my room to change."

Yakim nodded. "I'll do the same soon."

"It's a pity. I quite like the way you look."

Lucifer kissed Yakim's cheek, then disappeared into the hallway. Yakim heard him speak, and a few seconds later, Mel appeared.

His eyes widened as he took Yakim in. Yakim would never even think about punching him, but why did he and Roque have to stare at him?

"You look incredibly handsome," Mel said as he came closer. "Lucifer spoiled you?"

"He seems to think that having me dress like a human was important."

Mel snickered. "I bet he does."

"What does that mean?"

"I'm just teasing. I bet he can't wait to take those clothes off you rather than have you wear them, though."

Yakim had only thought about fitting better with Lucifer when he'd accepted the clothes, but the fact that Lucifer found him appealing when he wore them was a bonus. Maybe he *would* let Lucifer take them off his body.

Yakim groaned. How had he gone from being sure that nothing could ever happen between them to thinking about a future they would share?

"What was that for?" Mel asked, sounding worried.

"I want him," Yakim said. "I don't know what it means or what it'll look like once we're back in Hell, but I want him."

Mel's smile was soft. "Good. You deserve him. He's good for you."

Yakim hoped Mel was right. "But I have no idea what I'm doing. He's the king of Hell."

"And he doesn't care that you're not a prince or whatever kind of demon he usually dates. He likes you because of who you are."

"And I like him because of who he is, but how am I supposed to behave?"

"You know, I had no idea what I was in for when Berith and I got together, but I'm glad I didn't let it stop me."

"And *I* understand why this is so complicated for you," Roque added. He squeezed Yakim's shoulder. "If you decide you want to be with him, you're going to have to quit your job as a bodyguard and probably move out of the palace."

Yakim nodded. "Exactly."

"Well, I'll be sorry to lose you as a bodyguard, but we'll still be friends," Mel said. "That's never going to change, no matter where you live. But Roque is right. This is a big change for you. Just don't let the fear of not knowing what will happen next take this away from you. He really cares about you, and it's clear you care about him. Give yourself a chance to find a way to make it work, and give him a chance to show you how much he cares about you. In the end, that's what matters the most."

Yakim wouldn't have agreed a few months ago, but now he found himself thinking that Mel was right. He had an incredible opportunity with Lucifer. He could spend the rest of his life making the king of Hell happy and allowing him to do the same. It was scary, and Yakim had a lot of thinking to do, but maybe changing so much of his life would be worth it.

Chapter Thirteen

When Lucifer's phone vibrated on top of his desk, he snatched it without looking at who was calling. Only a few selected people had his number, and they were all people he wanted to hear from.

"Yes?"

"Your Highness," Bretton answered, his tone saying he was teasing.

Technically, he *should* be calling Lucifer *your Highness*, but Lucifer had ordered him not to long ago, and Bretton had always obeyed that order. It was the only one he'd ever obeyed, actually.

Bretton was one of the few who'd never hesitated to stand up to Lucifer, tell him when he was wrong, and even tell him to fuck off every so often. Lucifer liked it that way because they were more friends than king and personal assistant. He didn't want them to change, and he didn't think Bretton did.

"Tell me you have something," Lucifer said as he leaned back in his chair.

He looked at the open door of his office. He could hear the other three talking in the living room, and he'd join them soon, but Bretton had sent him a few documents he'd needed to go over, so he'd gone to his office.

"Beyond the documents I already sent you?"

"I'll only look them over once you tell me you found something."

Bretton snickered. "Yes, I have found something. In fact, I've found some*one*."

Lucifer sucked in a breath. "Really?"

"You sound like you didn't have a lot of faith in me."

"I did. If anyone could find him, I knew it'd be you. Considering what little we have to go on, I didn't expect anyone to be able to."

"I did a thing."

Bretton still wasn't apologetic, but he didn't need to be for Lucifer to know that whatever he'd done hadn't been approved of by him. "What did you do?"

"I tried to find Yakim's father with the little information you gave me, but I wasn't getting anywhere, so I contacted his mother."

Lucifer groaned and closed his eyes. "He's going to be angry when he finds out."

"From what she said, I doubt he will. She's certainly not going to contact him."

It was a pity. Lucifer wanted Yakim to have people who cared about him, and who better than his mother? But she didn't care, so it was better if she was out of Yakim's life. Lucifer would love him enough to make him forget that his mother wasn't in his life.

"I'm surprised she answered your questions."

"She didn't want to, but Berith can be convincing."

Of course Bretton had involved Berith. Lucifer wasn't even surprised. "What did she say?"

"She gave us a few more details, including an old address and the names of his parents, Yakim's grandparents. It was enough, and I have a current address."

"Send it to me."

"Already on its way. Do you think Yakim will want to go?"

"I know he will. He wants to see his father, whatever happens. I think he wants answers and closure."

"Understandable. You'll be going with him."

It wasn't a question, but Lucifer answered anyway. "Yes."

"Good. He shouldn't do this alone. I checked the man's social media, and he doesn't seem to be anti-demon, but there's no way to be sure."

"I'll keep Yakim safe."

"I know you will." Bretton hesitated. "I was against your relationship with him initially."

Lucifer snorted. "You could say that."

"I was afraid he'd be one of those demons who wanted something from you. I should have known better and trusted you, and I apologize for not doing so. It's clear the two of you care about each other, and it's good to see that you've finally found someone like that."

"Thank you. He's nothing like the people I had in my life before him, and I don't want to do anything that will ruin this."

"You'll find a way to make it work. You always do."

Bretton had faith in Lucifer, and Lucifer hoped it wasn't misplaced.

They hung up after talking about the documents Bretton had sent, and Lucifer got to his feet instantly. Bretton had promised he'd already sent an email, so Lucifer quickly opened the app to find it as he walked. His attention was on his phone when he entered the living room, but he heard the three stop talking, so he knew they were looking at him.

He glanced up, and his gaze caught Yakim's. "Bretton found him."

Yakim's eyes widened. "My father?"

"Yes. I have all the information in an email. From what Bretton said, your father doesn't seem to be anti-demon, but there's no way to know how he'll react to your presence and what you have to say."

Yakim got up from the couch. "That's fine. I'll deal with his reaction when it comes, but I want to see him."

He'd already said that before, but Lucifer had wondered if

it would change once the possibility of seeing his father got real. Clearly, that wasn't the case. Yakim looked more excited than Lucifer had ever seen him.

He prayed that Yakim's father would be the gentle and sweet person his son was. He didn't want Yakim to be hurt. He wanted to protect and shield him, but he needed to let Yakim make his own decisions in this situation.

And he'd decided to see his father.

"When are you going?" Mel asked.

"Right away," Yakim declared. He looked down at himself. "I need to get changed, but I'll be back soon," he promised.

He started to walk past Lucifer, only to stop and reach for him. Lucifer didn't expect Yakim to kiss him in front of his friends. He didn't usually, maybe because he was still hesitant in their relationship. But right now, he didn't seem to have a problem with it. His lips pressed against Lucifer's, leaving Lucifer breathless.

Then Yakim was gone.

"I hope his father deserves all this excitement," Mel murmured.

Lucifer looked at him. "Even if he doesn't, I'll make sure he treats Yakim right."

But even so, there was nothing Lucifer could do to control the man's words or reactions. For as much as he wanted to shield Yakim, he couldn't.

Yakim was nervous but wouldn't allow himself to think about it. He'd never thought the time would come when he'd meet his father, and no matter what happened, he wanted this to be over with. Once it was, he'd know one way or another and be able to go on with his life.

The chances that his father was horrible were high. A lot of humans disliked demons, even when they weren't open about it, and they would especially dislike it if one of them was their son. Yakim would be ready if that happened, but he found himself praying it wouldn't.

It might be foolish, but he wanted his father to be a good person. He wanted at least one of his parents to care about him. He didn't understand why. The parents of most of the demons he knew couldn't care less if they lived or died or what happened to them. That was how things usually were in Hell.

But it was changing. Yakim had seen demons fall in love, and just watching Berith and Mel was enough to tell him that demons *could* love. Surely, that love wasn't only romantic. Berith loved his daughter as much as he loved Mel, albeit in a different way. He was a good father. That had to mean that demons could love just like humans.

But if they could, it meant they *chose* not to love their children, like Yakim's mother. Yakim had always behaved as if he didn't care, but it still hurt. He didn't understand why she'd never told him about his father. Was it because he was even worse than her or because he was so much better? It was clear she hadn't wanted him to find his father, and he didn't know why, but until he found out, he'd be extremely nervous.

"Everything will be all right," Lucifer soothed. "Whatever happens, I'll be there."

They stood together on the sidewalk, staring at the building in front of them. Yakim had changed into the suit Lucifer had bought for him, but he felt ridiculous. It wasn't him, even though, in a way, it was. He liked the suit because of the way Lucifer had looked at him when he'd worn it the first time, but maybe it wasn't such a good idea to wear it when meeting his father. It might ruin the good feelings he had when he looked at himself wearing the suit, and he didn't want that to happen.

Yakim wanted to be appealing to Lucifer. He knew that it

had nothing to do with the suit, but he wanted to make Lucifer happy, just like the king made him happy.

He'd found his father for him. He hadn't hesitated to bring him to his father's place, and he'd be standing by his side when he met the man who had given him life. He'd be ready to step in, whatever Yakim needed, and that meant so much to Yakim. He could never thank Lucifer enough, but he didn't have to. This was what people who cared about each other did.

It was what people who *loved* each other did.

Because what Yakim and Lucifer had was love. Yakim had avoided it for a long time but couldn't anymore. He could see it in everything Lucifer did for him, and he wanted so much more. He wanted to give Lucifer everything he wished for, too, even though he didn't know where to start.

His job as a bodyguard had been important to him, and it still was, but he'd come to realize it wasn't as important as Lucifer. If he had to quit to be with the demon he loved, he would. He wouldn't even hesitate. He'd be sad, but it wouldn't stop him.

Lucifer pressed a hand against Yakim's back. "We can just head home. We can come back another time if it's too hard for you. You know where he lives now, so you can visit whenever you want."

It was tempting, but Yakim shook his head. "I want to do it now. If it goes badly, I want time to get over it before we go back to Hell, and if it goes well, I want enough time to visit again and get to know him."

"I understand. Are you ready to go inside, then?"

Yakim wasn't, but he nodded anyway. He allowed Lucifer to guide him into the building and the elevator. He had no idea where they were going. But Lucifer did, and Yakim trusted him with his life.

The building was nice. It wasn't luxurious or anything like

what Yakim was used to seeing at the palace, but it was clean and well-kept. It wasn't special, but it seemed like a good place to live.

Yakim hoped his father had a nice life. It didn't matter if he'd allowed Yakim's mother to take him away or if he'd pushed her to do so. Yakim could only imagine how hard it would have been for him to become a father to a half-demon who could never pass for a human.

They eventually stopped in front of a door on the third floor. Lucifer was still touching Yakim, and he looked at him in question. If Yakim shook his head or did anything that told Lucifer he wasn't ready for this, Lucifer would take him away. Yakim didn't think he'd ever be ready, but he wanted to do this.

He nodded, and Lucifer raised his hand to knock. Yakim held his breath as he waited. He could hear someone moving inside the apartment, and he tensed as the footsteps came closer. He released his breath when the door swung open, and he saw the man standing on the other side.

Yakim wasn't sure if he was fooling himself, but he could see that this man was his father. Their jaw had the same squarish form, and even though Yakim's eyes were white and his father's were brown, they were similar in form. Their hair was the same. Yakim's mother had straight hair that she grew long, and while Yakim cut his short, it was curly, like his father's.

Yakim knew that his father's name was Frank. It was one of the few things he'd gotten out of his mother. He hadn't known what to expect, but Frank seemed like a normal enough human. His graying curly hair was a bit messy and too long, and he wore glasses that partially shielded his tired eyes. He was shorter than Yakim, but Yakim was a demon, which meant he was taller than humans. His father wore a sweater and a pair of jeans, with white socks on his feet.

Frank's first reaction was to take a step back. His gaze jumped from Lucifer to Yakim, and while Yakim expected him to focus on Lucifer since he looked human, he didn't.

Frank squinted and cocked his head. He stared at Yakim as if he expected something, but Yakim wasn't sure he could speak even if he tried.

Lucifer cleared his throat. "We're looking for Frank."

"*I'm* Frank. What can I help you with?"

"My name is Yakim," Yakim blurted out. "You're my father."

That probably wasn't the best way to do this, but Yakim couldn't stop himself. He'd been waiting for this moment since he was a child, and it was finally happening.

His father stared at him for what felt like an eternity but couldn't have been more than a few seconds. "Fredelle is your mother?"

If Yakim had any doubts Frank was his father, they were gone. "She is."

Frank stepped forward, then stopped moving and stepped back into the apartment. Yakim couldn't help but wonder what he'd been about to do. Take a better look at him? Maybe hug him? Yakim wouldn't have known how to react, but he wanted to find out.

"Why don't you come in?" Frank asked.

His voice held no scorn or disgust, and Yakim told himself to relax. Even if his father wanted nothing to do with him after this, he didn't seem horrified by the fact that he had a demon child.

Yakim looked at Lucifer, who nodded. He was the first to walk into the apartment, and Yakim quickly followed. It should have been the other way around since he was supposed to protect Lucifer, but his lover would protect him in this situation.

And his heart.

To Yakim's surprise, Frank wasn't focused on Lucifer. He gestured at them to sit down in the small living room, and when they did, he sat on Yakim's side and leaned as close to him as possible without touching him.

"My name is Lucifer," Lucifer said, holding out a hand.

Frank stared at it for a moment as if it might bite him, but instead of shying away like Yakim expected, he eventually shook it.

"I was going to ask if Lucifer was a common name in Hell, but I'm afraid to find out the answer," he said.

"It is not," Lucifer said with a nod. "I'm the king of Hell."

Frank swallowed audibly. "And you're here with my son."

"I'm here to protect him in case he needs to be protected."

Great. Yakim's lover was already terrorizing his father, and they'd only just met.

Yakim's father seemed like a nice enough person. He hadn't screamed at them to leave. He hadn't told them to fuck off and that he didn't want demons in his apartment. Instead, he'd invited them in, and he seemed to be less afraid of Yakim than he was of Lucifer. Maybe Lucifer shouldn't have told him who he was, but if this man was going to be his father-in-law, he probably needed to know.

"I'm curious as to how my son became so close to the king of Hell," Frank said.

"We can answer your questions, but I'd like for you to answer his first," Lucifer told him.

He hoped Frank would turn his attention back to Yakim, and he was relieved when that was what happened.

It was almost like Frank couldn't look away from Yakim for long. Every time he glanced at Lucifer, it was only for a few seconds before his focus returned to Yakim. He didn't seem disgusted or anything like that. The meeting had started well, and Lucifer hoped it would end that way.

"I didn't think I'd ever see you again," Frank said.

Yakim leaned forward as if he wanted to be closer to his father. Frank hadn't offered them anything to drink, but Lucifer didn't mind. This meeting was about Yakim and Frank, not about him or how thirsty he was.

"So you know me? My mother never told me why she went back to Hell or when she did. I just knew I was born here, that my father was human, and that she took me to Hell when I was a baby, but that's it."

Frank's expression turned angry for a moment, but he quickly smoothed it out. that got Lucifer's attention. He was ready to intervene if necessary, but thankfully, it didn't look like Frank's anger was aimed at Yakim.

"I always knew your mother didn't love me," Frank said. "It was the first thing she said when we met. She told me that she could never love me because she was a demon, and demons don't love. I didn't care. She was beautiful, and I got to know her over the time we were together. It might sound stupid, but I fell in love with her. She never said anything about going back to Hell, and when she got pregnant with you, I thought it meant we'd stay together. She seemed settled in a way I'd never seen her before, and I fooled myself into thinking that this was it. I thought the pregnancy would fix all the problems we had."

"I'm guessing it didn't," Yakim murmured.

Frank shook his head. "She was fine until you were born. We tried to make it work, and I did everything I could to ensure she knew she was loved. I cared for you, even though I had no idea what to do with a baby. I could see she wasn't happy, but nothing I tried seemed to help. She never said anything to me. She certainly never mentioned taking you back to Hell. I think she believed I would have tried to stop her if she had."

"Would you have?"

"I don't know. I never wanted her to be unhappy, and I wouldn't have stopped her if it had been just her, but there was you to think about. I didn't want to give you up. I know I can't survive in Hell, but I could have tried to see you as much as I could. Divorced human parents make it work, and I hoped we could find a way to do the same."

"What happened?" Yakim's voice was little more than a whisper.

"One day, I came back from work, and you were both gone. You were only six months old. I'd thought I had all the time in the world with you, but I only had six months. I tried looking for both of you, but I already knew I wouldn't find you. Eventually, I had to give up, but I never gave up hope that we would find each other again." He paused. "You're really my son?"

Yakim nodded. "She never told me about you. She just gave me your name and the city in which you lived, but then she closed off and told me to stop asking questions. Even when I was a child, she never told me about you. I didn't even know if you were aware of my existence."

"I did, and I cherished the thought that you were growing up and living a happy life with her."

Yakim and Lucifer looked at each other. Lucifer wasn't about to say anything, and he wasn't surprised when Yakim didn't tell his father that his life hadn't been happy. He was happy now, but he'd grown up in Hell with a distant mother.

"I always hoped you'd find me again," Frank continued. "I can't believe you have. I have so many questions, and I'm sure you have just as many."

"I want us to get to know each other," Yakim said. "If that's something you want. I'll be in the human realm for a bit, so we can meet."

Frank's eyes were full of tears when he nodded. "I'd like

that."

Lucifer leaned back in his seat. He didn't care how long Yakim wished to stay here with Frank. He'd give him all the time he asked for, and when they had to leave, he'd promise both of them they could see each other again soon, even every day if they wanted.

Lucifer's father was an asshole, but Yakim's wasn't, and Yakim deserved to get to know him. Obviously, his father wanted the same, and for the first time, Lucifer allowed himself to hope that at least this would end up going the right way.

They stayed with Frank for several hours. It was clear that Frank and Yakim wanted to continue talking, but it was getting late. Eventually, Lucifer gave Frank his address, something he'd never done before. No human except Mel had ever been to the apartment. Frank would come, though, and that was fine with Lucifer.

It took about half an hour for Frank and Yakim to say goodbye, but eventually, Lucifer and Yakim found themselves on the street. Lucifer stayed quiet, not knowing how overwhelmed Yakim was. He no doubt needed time to wrap his mind around all of it, so as they made their way back home, Lucifer held his hand and stayed quiet. He'd give Yakim whatever he needed, including silence.

That was what he got when they reached the apartment. Lucifer remembered that Mel and Roque were having dinner with Mel's family tonight, which was a relief because it meant Yakim would have some space. If they'd been present, both of them would have wanted to know how it had gone, and that didn't seem to be what Yakim needed right now.

Lucifer closed the front door but didn't turn on the lights. Yakim stood close by, seemingly lost in thought. Lucifer gently touched his back.

"Everything all right?" he murmured.

Yakim turned toward him. "He never wanted me to leave. He wants to get to know me and seems like a good person."

"He does. I'm happy for you, Yakim."

Yakim stepped so close Lucifer could feel their bodies brushing against each other. "I wouldn't have any of this if it weren't for you. You brought me to the human realm and found my father."

"It was nothing," Lucifer said.

He was uncomfortable. He didn't want Yakim to feel he owed him. He'd done it because he was in love with him and wanted him to be happy, not because he expected anything from him.

Yakim stepped forward again, and Lucifer moved back. He hit the door, but he wasn't afraid, not even when Yakim caged him with his arms. He looked up at his lover, eager to find out where this was going.

Lucifer had seen Yakim smile before, but never like this. Yakim's smile was so wide it looked like he might hurt his cheeks if he didn't stop, and Lucifer found himself smiling back.

"I love you," Yakim said.

Lucifer gaped. He hadn't expected that, but he was ready for it. "I love you, too."

Yakim kissed Lucifer, and Lucifer knew that whatever happened next, no matter how many doubts and unknowns there were, they could get over them as long as they were together.

Yakim hadn't been planning on telling Lucifer he loved him today, but he didn't regret it. As long as he and Lucifer were together, he didn't think there was anything he would ever regret. He wanted Lucifer so much that sometimes he wondered how he'd lived before meeting the king of Hell.

He didn't want to remember. He just wanted to be with Lucifer, and by some miracle, Lucifer wanted to be with him. Yakim would never have imagined his life would go like this, but now that it had, he didn't want it to change. Whatever sacrifice he needed to make to be with Lucifer, he'd do it. Lucifer was more important than a job. He held Yakim's heart, and Yakim hoped he'd never give it back.

Lucifer felt perfect in his arms, but they couldn't stay here in the entrance. Eventually, Mel and Roque would come home, and while they already knew that Yakim and Lucifer were together, they didn't need to walk in on them making love against the door.

Stepping away from Lucifer felt like the hardest thing Yakim had done recently, but he did it anyway. He stared at Lucifer, unable to look away.

The king of Hell usually looked composed and had every single hair in place, but not tonight. Tonight, his hair was messed up from Yakim's hands, his cheeks were flushed, and his mouth hung slightly open. He stared back at Yakim with wide eyes that told Yakim that, just like him, he wanted more.

Yakim took Lucifer's hand and dragged him toward the bedroom. Lucifer laughed, not resisting for even one second. They both wanted the same thing.

Yakim didn't think he'd ever be able to thank Lucifer enough for what he'd done. He'd not only found his father. He'd also allowed him to meet Frank and spend time with him, something Yakim had never expected to happen. He didn't understand why Lucifer loved him and wanted his happiness, but he didn't really care. As long as Lucifer was in his arms and his life, he no longer cared about the reason.

Lucifer was on him as soon as the bedroom door closed behind them. He grabbed Yakim's horns and pulled on them so that Yakim would lower his body. Then he kissed him. Yakim's hands landed on Lucifer's hips, and he hauled him closer to his body. Lucifer was short compared to Yakim, so it wasn't a surprise when he tried to climb up Yakim's body.

Yakim helped him by grabbing his ass and lifting him. Lucifer wrapped his legs around Yakim's waist, holding on for dear life as Yakim's back hit the wall. Lucifer squeaked, and Yakim turned them around so that Lucifer was against the wall.

He felt Lucifer's feet move, then heard the sound of his shoes hitting the floor. They were wearing too much to do anything Yakim wanted to do, but it was hard to give Lucifer space when Yakim never wanted to let go of him.

Lucifer wiggled again. His legs' hold on Yakim's waist loosened, and Yakim took the opportunity to unhook his lover from his body. Lucifer opened his mouth, possibly to argue, but Yakim didn't give him the opportunity to do so. He put Lucifer on his feet, then turned him around and pushed him against the wall.

Lucifer squeaked but didn't try to fight Yakim. Yakim was very much aware of how powerful his lover was and of the fact that Lucifer could kill him with a thought if he did something he didn't want. It was one of the reasons Yakim didn't have to worry about doing something Lucifer disliked. Lucifer wouldn't be shy about telling him, and if his mouth was otherwise occupied and he couldn't say the words, he'd find another way.

Yakim reached around Lucifer and found his belt. Lucifer sucked in a breath and pressed his cheek against the wall, and Yakim took a moment to look at him as he unfastened his belt, then his dress pants.

As soon as they were both undone, Lucifer's pants slid down his body to land around his ankles. Yakim didn't take them off. Instead, he plastered his body against Lucifer's back, sure that his lover could feel how aroused he was. His fingers found the head of Lucifer's cock peeking from under the elastic of his underwear, and he gently played with it for a moment. It was sticky, and it made Yakim's mouth water.

He slid his other hand up and under Lucifer's shirt. His fingers found one nipple, and he played with it as he pushed Lucifer's underwear under his balls. They didn't fall down, but now, Yakim had better access to Lucifer's cock, which was what he'd wanted.

Lucifer moaned. His cheek was still pressed against the wall, so Yakim could see half of his face. Yakim didn't think he'd ever been so beautiful. It wasn't only the way he looked but also the fact that he'd surrendered. Yakim couldn't imagine Lucifer allowing just anyone to see him like this, and he was touched by Lucifer's trust in him. He'd never betray it, and he hoped Lucifer knew that.

Yakim dropped to his knees. Lucifer made a strangled sound and tried pushing away from the wall, but Yakim splayed a hand against his back and pushed him back into position. Once he was sure Lucifer wouldn't move, he used both hands to slide Lucifer's underwear down his legs until they joined the pants around his ankles. Lucifer wasn't naked, but he might as well be. His ass was right there, calling for Yakim.

Yakim answered.

He pried apart Lucifer's ass cheeks. He was slightly hairy here, and since they'd showered before leaving the apartment, Yakim didn't hesitate to lean closer. He rubbed his nose against one meaty ass cheek, then delved in between them, giving a tentative lick. Lucifer swore, and Yakim grinned against his hole.

He was going to drive Lucifer nuts.

He licked again, using his hands to hold Lucifer in place. He didn't think Lucifer would push him away, and once Lucifer started pushing back as if he wanted more, Yakim let go. With his face buried into Lucifer's ass, Yakim was in heaven.

He didn't care that heaven probably didn't exist. He just knew that he never wanted this moment to end.

He wrapped one hand around Lucifer's cock and played with it as he ate out his lover. Lucifer continued swearing and babbling, and Yakim focused on giving him as much pleasure as he could. He wanted Lucifer to be unable to live without him, just like he was unable to live without Lucifer.

"Get in me," Lucifer croaked.

Yakim leaned back. "I need something to ease the way in." Yakim was much taller than Lucifer and proportionate everywhere, including his dick.

"I'll take care of it. Just fuck me, please."

Lucifer trusted Yakim, and Yakim trusted him. If Lucifer said he would take care of it, Yakim knew he would.

He rose to his feet and grabbed Lucifer's hips. He held him close as he let go with one hand and quickly opened his dress pants. He wished he were faster, but he'd lose these pants if he didn't wear a belt, and he'd wanted to look nice to meet his father.

Eventually, the pants hit the floor. He wasn't planning on going anywhere, so he left them where they were and wrapped his fingers around his cock. He didn't want to hurt Lucifer, so he teased Lucifer's hole with his thumb. His eyes went wide when he felt the slickness there. He'd opened Lucifer as much as he could have with his tongue, but there was no way this was because of him.

He pushed his thumb inside, making Lucifer keen. He tried pushing back, but Yakim was in charge, and he didn't let him. Instead, he took his thumb out, hooked an arm around Lucifer's waist, and hauled him higher against the wall. He pressed his body against him so he wouldn't slide down and aimed his cock to the entrance of his lover's body.

He was careful as he entered him. No matter how much slickness he could feel, he'd never forgive himself if he hurt

Lucifer in any way. Pinned like this to the wall, Lucifer couldn't push back, which meant Yakim was in charge of how quickly and how deep he went.

He ignored Lucifer's begging to just fuck him now and took his time. Once he was fully inside his lover, he pressed his body against Lucifer's back, plastering him against the wall. He pinned him there with his hips, then used one of his hands to raise Lucifer's leg. It gave him better access, but it still wasn't entirely comfortable because every time he moved back to fuck into Lucifer, Lucifer's body slid down the wall.

This wasn't going to work.

Still inside Lucifer, Yakim grabbed his hips and stepped away from the wall. He stumbled and remembered that he hadn't taken off his pants. He wasn't about to put Lucifer down, so he slid one foot out of the pants with his shoe still on. That was enough to allow him to walk. He kept Lucifer impaled on his cock as he moved them to the bed. Once there, he lowered down, and Lucifer quickly got his knees under him. With their height difference, it still wasn't entirely comfortable, but it was easier to fuck him.

Which was precisely what Yakim did.

Lucifer's body was tight and warm around him. Between that and the sounds Lucifer made, Yakim doubted he'd need much more stimulation to come, but he wanted Lucifer to come first. He pressed one hand against the mattress by Lucifer's head and wrapped his other arm around Lucifer's waist, holding him in place as he slammed into him. His fingers found Lucifer's cock, and he pulled on it, grinning at the sound Lucifer made. Lucifer was still wearing his shirt, so when Yakim went to bite his shoulder, he had to bite through it.

That seemed to do the trick. Lucifer shouted, and his body tensed. His ass squeezed around Yakim's cock, and Yakim bit harder as he allowed himself to come and fill Lucifer's body, leaving a part of him as deep inside of Lucifer as he could.

For a moment, the room was silent except for the sound of both of them panting. It was as if time had stopped, and Yakim squeezed his eyes shut. If this was how sex between them would be every time, he was pretty sure he'd die of a heart attack in just a few years.

What a way to go.

CHAPTER FOURTEEN

They'd been in the human realm for a few weeks now, and everything was perfect. Lucifer was spending more time than he could ever have thought possible with Yakim, exploring the city and spoiling him in a way he'd never been spoiled. Mel had seen his family almost every day since they'd arrived, and he was clearly enjoying himself.

But it couldn't last forever.

Mel was making noises about returning to the palace because he missed Berith, and while Lucifer didn't want their little bubble to explode, he knew Mel was right. Mel had been away from the palace long enough, and people would start talking if the consort didn't return soon. Besides, Lucifer had had enough of hiding. He'd enjoyed the vacation, but he wanted to start his new life with Yakim, and that wouldn't happen if they kept hiding in the human realm.

Being here had given three of them something they wanted. Mel had seen his family, Lucifer had been with Yakim, and Yakim had contacted his father and was getting to know him. It was time for things to change, though, and that would only happen if Lucifer finally took charge.

Bretton and Berith had been working on finding out more about the people trying to kill Lucifer, but Lucifer felt they were being too cautious. He already knew who wanted to kill him and was ready to face them. He had enough of hiding and couldn't stay here forever, anyway.

Bretton had insisted they had to return to the palace because people needed to see Lucifer, and that hadn't changed.

Lucifer would have already gone back if the situation had been different, and he was ready for it.

He wasn't sure where the others stood, so he brought it up at breakfast.

"I thought it would be a good idea for us to return to Hell," he declared.

Mel smiled instantly, but Yakim was more hesitant. Roque didn't seem to care one way or the other, probably because he didn't have anything tying him to the human realm.

Lucifer had expected Yakim to be hesitant because of his father, so he was surprised when that wasn't the case.

"Things could still be dangerous for you in Hell. It would be better to let Bretton and Berith find out who's behind the society and take care of them before you return."

Lucifer was so much in love with his demon. He wasn't thinking about himself and what he'd lose if he went back to Hell. He was focused on Lucifer.

Lucifer reached over the table to squeeze one of Yakim's hands. "They've been working on it, and we're pretty sure we already know who's behind it. They can't do anything unless I'm there, though. Besides, I'm tired of hiding. I want us to start our life together, and we can't do that from here."

Yakim slowly nodded. "I understand. I'm just worried."

Lucifer wanted to tell him he didn't have to be. Lucifer was the strongest demon in Hell. He could take down demons taller and stronger than him. Some people didn't understand that because they'd never seen him using his powers, and when he thought about it, he realized that Yakim hadn't, either. He'd seen some of it but not all, and maybe knowing more about what Lucifer could do would help him.

"I assure you I can defend myself," Lucifer told him. "I can show you if you want. I'm not only powerful. I'm also trained in combat, so I can kick anyone's ass if they try anything."

Yakim rolled his eyes. "I already know you can defend

yourself. There's no need to brag."

"I'm not bragging. I'm trying to reassure you, since it's clear you're worried."

"I am, but it doesn't mean I don't have faith in you. I just wish we knew more about the society and what they're planning."

"I don't think it's possible for us to find out more from here. Bretton and Berith have done everything they can. They tried convincing me to stay when I last talked to them, but I don't believe it's advisable. We need to do something, and we need to do it soon." Lucifer leaned closer to Yakim. "I want us to start our life together. I want to find a palace we like and move there. I want to stop worrying about what the society is doing."

Yakim sighed. "I get it. You're not wrong, and I want the same. I'm just worried."

"I don't blame you for being worried, but I want you to trust me."

"I do trust you," Yakim said instantly.

That made Lucifer feel better. He looked around the table. "What do you think? Should we continue hiding here?"

"Well, I'm ready to go home," Mel said. "And I know I could go back whenever I want, but I don't want to leave you here. But we go back together or don't go back at all."

Lucifer was touched, but he thought it wasn't necessary. He didn't need Mel here to defend him, but it felt good to be supported and to know that, like Berith, Mel was there if he needed anything. It didn't matter that Mel was young and human. Lucifer welcomed all kinds of support and help.

He glanced at Roque, who shrugged. They wouldn't get anything else from him.

It was down to Yakim.

Lucifer returned his attention to him. "Look, I understand you're worried, and I know that no matter how many times I tell you not to be, it's not going to change. You have good reasons to be worried. We can't stay here forever, though. If we don't go back, my father and sister will try to take over. They want the throne, and killing me would have been the easiest way to get it, but they won't have to kill me if I don't go back and people don't see me. They can take the throne just by pointing out that I'm not a good king because I'm not even in Hell."

Yakim rubbed his forehead. "I guess I'm going to have to get used to this."

"To dating a king and thinking like one? Yes, you will. You don't have to do so now, though. Leave everything to me."

"I'm not going to let you face all of this on your own."

"I don't expect you to. I'll do the thinking, and you can protect me like you always do."

"Didn't you just say you didn't need protection?"

Lucifer could tell Yakim was teasing. He was still worried, too, and Lucifer didn't want to dismiss that fear. "I can defend myself, but you can defend me, too. There's no one I would trust more with my safety than you. Together, we can make this work, and we will."

"What about my father?"

"You can see him anytime you want. Just tell me, and I'll create a portal that will bring you straight to his living room."

"You don't have to do that."

"Maybe not, but I *want* to do it."

This wasn't the best place to do this, especially with Mel and Roque at the table with them, but Lucifer didn't want to wait. He squeezed Yakim's hand and leaned closer, pressing a kiss to his cheek.

"I'd do pretty much anything for you," he said, his voice barely more than a whisper. "That's why I want to go back. Going back means retaking control, and that means you'll be safe. It means we can start our life together, and there's nothing I want more. I realize you have a lot of thinking to do, and there will be many changes in your life, but until I'm ready not to be king anymore, that's unfortunately not going to change. I don't want to force you into anything, but I can't ignore what my father and my sister are doing. If I don't want to lose the throne and Hell, I need to go back."

"Don't worry about me. I might have to give up being a bodyguard, but I get you in exchange, and that's more than enough."

Lucifer wasn't sure it was, but he wouldn't argue. If Yakim wanted him enough to leave the palace he considered his home and the people he considered family, he wouldn't stop him. Besides, it wasn't like they were going far.

Bretton might not have succeeded in finding out enough about the society, but he'd finally found a new palace for Lucifer, and Lucifer couldn't wait. He wanted to show it to Yakim and to move him there, but before doing so, the society needed to be extirpated from his court.

And it was finally time to do just that.

Yakim didn't like the idea of Lucifer being back in Hell, but he understood what Lucifer was saying. He was the king, and he couldn't hide forever. His place was on the throne, not in the human realm. No matter how little Yakim liked it, they were going back.

Mel got to his feet. "I'm going to start packing."

His eagerness made Yakim smile. Mel could have gone back anytime he wanted, but he'd refused, saying he wished to visit his family for longer. Everyone around the table knew that wasn't really why he was still there. He didn't want to leave Yakim and Lucifer behind. He was loyal to them, even though there was nothing he could do in this situation. Yakim knew how much that meant to Lucifer, which was one of the reasons he wasn't arguing.

Everyone but him wanted to go back.

The main reason he didn't was his father. They'd been talking almost every day, although they hadn't seen each other often enough. Frank had to work, so it wasn't always easy, but he'd made an effort to spend time with Yakim and get to know him, and Yakim was touched. He'd expected a monster, but instead, he'd found a parent. He might never have had his mother, but he had his father, and that meant everything.

He might argue more if he didn't know that Lucifer would open a portal anytime Yakim wanted to see Frank. Lucifer spoiled him, and not just because he bought him things. He wanted Yakim to be happy, and sometimes, it still stunned Yakim to realize that.

No one had wanted him to be happy before. His mother certainly hadn't, and while Berith was a friend, Yakim worked for him. He wanted Yakim happy, but his safety and the safety of the people he loved came first. But Yakim wasn't just a bodyguard anymore. He was with Lucifer, which would entail many changes, not only because Yakim would have to quit his job.

He wasn't an idiot. He knew Lucifer wanted him to be his consort, and while the thought terrified him, he didn't think there was a way out. Being Lucifer's consort meant climbing up Hell's hierarchy and ending up above Berith, which wasn't something Yakim wanted to consider. He had no idea what to do as the king's consort, but he supposed he would find out.

As soon as the society was dealt with.

Mel had already vanished into the bedroom he'd used while they were here, and Roque wasn't far behind. That left Yakim and Lucifer in the kitchen to clean up.

"You're sure you want to do this?" Lucifer asked.

"I am, so stop worrying. I'm not letting you go back by

yourself."

Lucifer shook his head. "I meant everything else. Your life is going to change if you want to continue being with me once we're back. I know you enjoy your job as a bodyguard and that you love your life as it is."

Yakim snatched him around the waist and pulled him closer. Lucifer almost fell off his chair, but Yakim dragged both him and the chair toward him. He wrapped his arms around Lucifer, and for a moment, he just breathed in his scent.

"I know things will change, but that's all right. I'm terrified, but as long as it means I can have you, I'm okay with it. I'm not going to change my mind or resent you for this. I'm making my own decisions, and you have better things to worry about than me."

"I don't think I'll ever be able to stop worrying about you."

"The same goes for me, but we have to trust each other. We can do this."

They had to.

Everything went quickly after that. By the time they were done cleaning the kitchen, Mel had finished packing his things and was bouncing on the balls of his feet. Lucifer would have someone come to clean the apartment, so they didn't have to worry about that. Yakim had the time to call his father to warn him that he was going back to Hell and to reassure him that they'd see each other soon, and then, they were gone.

Lucifer opened the portal from his living room to the portal room at the palace. The place was empty, as it should be, and instead of allowing the two guards by the doors to go ahead and warn the prince that he was back, Mel was so eager to see Berith that he ran down the hallway. Roque went after him with a laugh. Yakim and Lucifer were slower, almost as if Lucifer wanted to enjoy his last moments alone with Yakim.

They'd have many of these moments, but it would be a while. Right now, they had problems to solve.

"Ready to do this?" Lucifer asked.

"I've never been more ready to do anything. We can do this."

Lucifer nodded. "Together."

It was strange to be a part of a *together*, especially with the king of Hell, but Lucifer was right. They were together now, and that was how they'd face their problems.

Mel had already vanished into Berith's office by the time Yakim and Lucifer reached it. Lucifer wasn't surprised. Mel had been eager to come back, and Lucifer suspected that he hadn't asked to do so because he'd wanted to support Yakim and Lucifer. It was sweet, but it had been unnecessary.

They were all back now, and it was time to finish this fight. Lucifer had had enough of the society. He'd had enough of his sister and his father threatening him from afar. He was ready to start his new life with Yakim, and the only way to make that happen would be to face them.

He and Yakim walked into the office after Lucifer quickly knocked on the open door. He wasn't surprised to find Berith sitting behind his desk with Mel in his lap. They were wrapped around each other, which left Bretton, who was sitting in front of Berith's desk, looking extremely uncomfortable. He appeared relieved to see Lucifer, probably because it gave him something else to focus on.

"Welcome back," he said, getting to his feet and lightly bowing. "I didn't expect you."

"It was a spur-of-the-moment decision," Lucifer explained. "I've had enough of hiding from my father and sister, and everyone agreed we should come home."

"Not everyone," Yakim grumbled.

He'd put down the bags in the corner of the room and had come to stand behind Lucifer. Lucifer didn't like that. Yakim was acting as his bodyguard, but they were so much more than that.

Lucifer reached back and grabbed one of Yakim's hands. He pulled him closer and wrapped his arm around Yakim's waist. He felt Yakim's body tense, but Yakim didn't pull away or say anything. Eventually, he relaxed, and Lucifer turned his attention back to Bretton.

He was watching them with an arched brow. He didn't appear surprised to see them together, and Lucifer hoped his friend wasn't going to scold him for distracting his bodyguard or something like that.

"Well, you should have called before deciding to come back. I don't have anything concrete on your father and sister," he said instead.

Lucifer sighed. "I'm not surprised." He let go of Yakim and went to sit in one of the empty chairs. Berith and Mel were still focused on each other, which meant Lucifer had time for Bretton and what he had to tell him. "What did you find out?"

"The usual. They've been talking to a lot of different people, and there are rumors, but I don't have any proof. I found out that your father is funneling money from the palace's accounts into his, so you'll want to do something about that, but I haven't found where that money is going."

Lucifer rolled his eyes. "He's using it to fund the society. Anything else?"

"Your sister has been making a lot of noise about becoming queen, but again, that's not new or surprising. You can't arrest her because she wants to be queen."

Couldn't he? Lucifer had always tried to be just in his role as king. He disliked using violence to obtain what he wanted or to punish people who deserved it. The palace had an extensive jail, and he'd filled many of its cells. He didn't want his subjects to be afraid of him, not even the ones who threatened his throne or his life.

But maybe, in this case, he could make an exception.

As the king, he had absolute power and the last word regarding this kind of decision. He didn't like having so much power without checks, which was one of the reasons he was always careful when he made decisions. He had enough of the society, though. He didn't need proof to confront his sister and father, and he was ready to get straight to the point.

"I've decided I'll go back as soon as possible," he declared. "I want to confront them. If you can find proof of their involvement, that's good, but even if you can't, I'm done waiting for the society to make their next move."

Bretton was already shaking his head. "That's a bad idea. I know that as king, you can do what you want, but they'll use it against you."

"Then find a way around it," Lucifer snapped. He sucked in a breath. "I apologize. I realize this isn't your fault, but I've had enough of them. I want to move closer and start my life with Yakim, and I feel I can't do that until I've taken care of them."

"Wait," Berith said, finally emerging from his embrace with Mel. "What do you mean you want to move closer?"

Lucifer looked at Bretton. "Haven't you told him?"

Bretton was carefully not looking at Berith. "I thought you'd want to do so yourself."

Lucifer snickered. So Bretton had been afraid to tell Berith about his new palace. "Before leaving, I told Bretton I was planning to move closer. Even after I lock up my father and sister and get rid of the rest of the society, I don't want to live at the palace. I'll carefully select the members of the court I want to come with me, and we'll start a new one here in your territory."

Berith stared. "You'd mentioned something, but I thought

Bretton had changed your mind."

Did Berith not want Lucifer so close? It wouldn't be a surprise. After all, Lucifer was talking about invading part of his territory. "That was before Yakim and I got together. We can go somewhere else, but I'd rather stay close, especially for Yakim's sake. I'm taking him away from his job and the people he considers family."

"Please leave me out of this," Yakim muttered from behind Lucifer.

Lucifer ignored him. He understood that Yakim was in an odd position. He was Lucifer's lover and would eventually be his consort, but at the same time, he was still one of Berith's guards. It couldn't be easy for him to deal with that or to make sense of it.

"I'd love to see you more often, and I don't care about you being in my territory," Berith said. "I just wonder how you're going to move so many people."

"As I said, they won't all be moving. Bretton will select only the people loyal to me."

Bretton grumbled, but Lucifer ignored him. This was what his personal assistant lived for. He loved challenges, and this would be one.

"Well, good luck with that." Berith grinned. "And if you need anything, you know where to find us. I'm not happy you're taking away one of my best bodyguards, but Yakim is more family than a guard. I want him to be happy, so make sure you do that."

Lucifer turned in his seat to look at Yakim. His cheeks were flushed, and he wasn't looking at either of them, but a smile played on his lips. Lucifer knew he'd been afraid of how Berith would take the fact that he was leaving him, so it was good that he'd been there when Berith had said he was happy for him.

"I can't say I expected you to fall in love with one of my

bodyguards," Berith continued.

Lucifer grinned at him. "I didn't, either, but this is the best thing that has ever happened to me. I want to make him happy because it means I'll be happy, too. Moving to a new palace, cleaning up the court, and being closer to you are all part of that plan."

And Lucifer would do everything in his power to make it happen as quickly as possible. He was done letting his father and his sister ruin his happiness. He was the king of Hell, and it was time he started acting accordingly when it came to them.

CHAPTER FIFTEEN

Yakim was worried. Lucifer had decided to rush into this because he wanted them to start their life together, but that didn't mean things would go well or that it was the right way to do it.

Lucifer did need to deal with his father and his sister if they were involved with the society, but rushing into this might be a mistake, and Yakim didn't want anything bad to happen. He would never forgive himself if something did that wouldn't have if Lucifer hadn't been distracted by him. He wasn't sure how to make Lucifer see that, though.

But he couldn't deny he was pleased. Even in his wildest dreams, he would never have thought he and the king of Hell would be together. He certainly hadn't imagined that Lucifer would move all the way to Berith's territory to make him happy. Yakim hadn't even had to ask.

Since they'd arrived back at the palace, Bretton had selected a few palaces for them to visit. Lucifer wanted Yakim to be part of the decision, but Yakim wouldn't know where to start choosing a palace. Lucifer had assured him they could make any changes they wanted, but Yakim's mind was stuck on the fact that the palace would be his. Well, his and Lucifer's, but still.

He'd be in charge. Lucifer had enough to focus on since he was the king of Hell, and the traditional role of his concert was to keep the palace under control. It would be easier if they moved everyone they trusted to this new place while leaving Lucifer's enemies behind, but people would talk. They'd imply that Yakim didn't know how to be a consort, maybe that he was weak because he was half human and that he'd used his body to seduce Lucifer.

He didn't care.

He had wild dreams of him and Lucifer leaving a happy life and of his father moving into the palace with them. Mel could live here because he was linked to Berith. Mel wore a bracelet that made it possible for him to survive, and the same could be done for Yakim's father. Yakim hadn't spoken to him about it, and he wasn't planning to do so until the palace was safe and everything was ready, but it was in the back of his mind.

He was surprised to realize he missed his father. They'd seen each other several times when he'd been in the human realm, and now that he wasn't there, his father tried to at least text him every day. They called each other a few times a week and talked for hours, and even though Yakim had never expected this kind of relationship with him, it filled his heart with love and happiness. He only had Frank back because of Lucifer, and he wanted to give Lucifer anything he'd ever dreamed of.

Apparently, that was a life with Yakim and a new palace closer to Berith's.

But while Bretton and Lucifer were focused on their new palace, Yakim was focused on the people who would be moving with them. He wouldn't be the head of security, and he didn't think he'd want to be and have that responsibility on his shoulders, but that was one position that needed to be filled by someone he trusted. He'd already asked Roque, but his friend had declined. He wanted to stay with Mel and continue protecting him, which Yakim didn't blame him for. If it was possible, he'd do the same.

It wasn't, so while Lucifer and Bretton made lists of people Lucifer was sure he could trust and wanted to bring along,

Yakim had been working on a list of demons he trusted who would be good heads of security. He hoped Lucifer wouldn't see it as him overstepping. He didn't think so, but there was only one way for him to find out.

He needed to talk to Lucifer.

It wasn't as daunting as it had been before, but it still wasn't easy. Yakim was trying to find his footing in their relationship, and it felt odd to know that sometimes he'd have to stand up to the king of Hell. Lucifer would never hurt him or anything like that, but he was used to getting what he wanted and being obeyed. The only one who regularly challenged him was Bretton, and he was still alive, so Yakim had high hopes.

"I know I should focus on my father and sister, but I can't stop looking at these pictures," Lucifer said from the couch.

He was holding a tablet and going through the many pictures Bretton had taken of the few palaces he'd found that would be suitable for Lucifer. The way he lounged on the couch made it obvious he was comfortable. He felt safe in Berith's palace, and Yakim wanted him to feel the same in the palace he'd call home soon.

"I don't believe you should focus on your family until you have everything in line," Yakim told him. "Like your head of security. Do you trust the one you have at the palace?"

Lucifer put down the tablet and looked up at him. "I know you want to be the head of security, but you can't."

He sounded worried, and Yakim didn't want him to be. "That's fine. I never expected to become head of security, especially not head of *your* security. I'll be your consort, and those two things don't go together."

"You will?" Lucifer sounded genuinely surprised.

"What else could I be? You and I are a couple, and we'll be living together as soon as you choose one of these palaces. Or did you want me to be your lover on the side?" They hadn't talked about it, and they should have. Yakim didn't think he could stand to the side and watch Lucifer marry someone else, even though it would be someone more suitable to become the king's consort.

To be honest, he couldn't imagine marrying Lucifer either, and he wondered if it was necessary. Mel and Berith hadn't married. Everyone treated Mel as a consort because Berith had made an announcement, but they hadn't held a ceremony. Of course, Berith was a prince of Hell, while Lucifer was the king, so it could be different.

Lucifer dropped his tablet on the couch and quickly got up. "What are you talking about? I don't expect you to be my lover. I don't want anyone but you, and if you say yes, I want you to be my consort. I just didn't think you'd even want to hear about it. You were so freaked out initially."

"I didn't think we'd last or that I could be your consort, but I don't want anyone else, either. I certainly don't want to see *you* with anyone else."

"Then you'll be my consort." Lucifer reached for Yakim and pulled him into his arms. He was much shorter, so he was the one who slotted himself against him, but it felt right.

Yakim kissed the top of Lucifer's head. "So that's something we probably should have talked about sooner."

Lucifer snickered. "We should have, but we have now, and everything is fine."

"Between us, yes, but what about everything else? I don't think you should move into the new palace until you have someone you trust will protect you. Tell me about your head of security."

Lucifer sighed, but Yakim knew he'd go along with what he'd asked. He loved Yakim and wished to give him what he wanted.

There was nothing Yakim wanted more than to protect Lucifer.

Lucifer understood why Yakim was worried. He wanted to promise that everything would be all right and that neither of them would be attacked, but he couldn't. Knowing his family, he was sure they'd try to find a way into the new palace, which was why Lucifer needed to get rid of them before moving.

The most important thing to him was to protect Yakim. Now that Yakim had accepted the fact that he'd be Lucifer's consort, Lucifer had to resist the urge to wrap him up in a blanket and keep him close all day, every day. He had to remember that Yakim had been independent his entire life and that he could defend himself, even once he wasn't a bodyguard anymore.

That would be an adjustment for both of them. Lucifer had never had a consort, and Yakim had never been anything more than a bodyguard. He'd done such a good job protecting Berith and his family. Doing so was in his blood. It would be hard for him to move on, especially to being the king's consort. Now, he had people protecting him. He'd have to follow their orders and do a job he'd never expected.

He was giving up so much for Lucifer, and Lucifer was humbled. Even though Yakim wouldn't be his head of security, the least he could do was listen to his doubts and his advice. Yakim knew what he was doing when it came to his security. Lucifer didn't.

"I honestly don't know if I trust him," he said, thinking about the head of security of his palace. "I don't think he'd hurt me or anyone else on purpose, but I've always thought he was kind of lazy. He used to be a great worker, but not so much anymore."

Lucifer didn't know what had changed. Maybe it was just that the man was getting older. If that was the case and he wanted to retire, Lucifer would ensure he had enough money to do so. The man had protected him for years.

But maybe this move meant that Lucifer could get fresh people in the key assignments of his court. He could get a new head of security, new bodyguards—he really needed those after what happened to the last two—and new everyone who came in close contact with him. He'd only keep the few people he trusted with his life, but everyone else would go. He'd give them enough money to live on until they found a new job, but that was it. If he didn't trust them, he didn't want them around Yakim.

Yakim nodded. "I'll have to look into it. I asked Roque if he wanted to work for you, but he'd rather stay here."

Lucifer wasn't surprised. He was sad for Yakim because he knew how important Roque was to him, but they weren't going far. Roque and Yakim could see each other anytime they wanted.

Lucifer would make sure of that.

Yakim had never been spoiled by his parents. He hadn't had the opportunity with his father, and his mother had been a typical demon, not giving him much love. It could have been worse, but Yakim hadn't been happy, and now, he would be. Lucifer would make sure he never regretted being with him. Becoming Lucifer's consort was a big sacrifice for Yakim. Lucifer never wanted him to regret it.

He wanted to confront his father and his sister, which was why he'd come back to Hell, but instead, Bretton had convinced him to stay with Berith for a while longer. He'd gone back alone, and Lucifer had no doubt he was working hard to find the proof he felt they needed. Lucifer had tried to convince him to do without, but Bretton had snapped that Lucifer wasn't his father and he needed to do this the right way. If they wanted to change Hell and how the demons behaved, Lucifer had to be the first to do so. He had to show everyone it could be done and be an example, and while it was annoying, Bretton was right.

Lucifer didn't care about his family and what happened to them, but everyone was watching him. They always did. They'd take note of how he treated them and what happened to them, and they'd decide if they should give their loyalty to Lucifer or someone else.

It needed to be him. That was the only way to change Hell and keep Yakim safe.

CHAPTER SIXTEEN

"What do you think of this one?" Lucifer asked as he stood in the middle of what could be his next throne room. He opened his arms and twirled, smiling at the exasperated look on Yakim's face.

"I thought you'd already chosen a palace. Isn't that what Bretton did while we were away?" Yakim asked.

"He did choose one, but I want to ensure I reviewed every option. Whatever we choose will be our home."

Yakim stared for a moment before sighing. He put his hands on his hips and looked up at the ceiling and the room around him.

Lucifer liked it. It was much smaller than Lucifer's throne room at his old palace, but he didn't need a bigger one. That one was massive because of how many people were in his court, but his new court wouldn't be like that. He'd never liked having to sit on his throne and being gawked at. The fewer people who were here, the better it would be for him. He'd feel less like he was a show they were staring at.

This was the second palace they'd visited today. Lucifer had been trying to distract both himself and Yakim, and he'd managed. At the very least, he hadn't thought about what Bretton was doing back at their old palace, which, as far as he was concerned, was a win.

He didn't like the thought of Bretton being over there alone. It was dangerous, especially since he was looking into Lucifer's sister and father. They had to know that Lucifer was wary of them and suspected them of being involved with the society. Even if they weren't, if they caught Bretton, they'd know for sure that Lucifer was up to something. Bretton didn't do anything important without Lucifer's approval. Spying on Lucifer's family qualified as important.

"It's better than the last one," Yakim admitted. "And I like the garden better in this one. I don't think your suite is big enough, though."

Lucifer hummed as he thought back to the suites they'd seen earlier. "We could choose another one. There are plenty."

"But that suite is the only one with a big bathtub, and it's the easiest to defend in case the palace is invaded."

Lucifer had to suppress a smile. He liked that Yakim was thinking like himself and worrying about being able to defend Lucifer, but also that he'd started thinking about more, like the bathtub. "We could tear down some walls and include the suite next to ours. I think whoever lived here before didn't share a room with their spouse. That's probably why the two main suites are smaller. We could make a massive one out of it since I intend to keep you in my bed as much as I can."

Yakim arched a brow. "Do you?"

Lucifer prowled toward him. Yakim watched him coming, a smile playing on his lips. When Lucifer reached him, Yakim's arms went around his body almost automatically. They were always touching if they were close enough, and Lucifer couldn't help but wonder how he'd survived without this. He felt like every time he wasn't touching Yakim was a waste. Having Yakim touch him often had made him realize how much he'd missed it.

Plenty of people touched him every day, but no one he trusted the way he trusted Yakim. It felt good not to have to worry if the person touching his hair was going to try slashing his throat. He didn't have to worry about Yakim gossiping behind his back about his five wives or whatever interested the court these days.

"I'm not going to ask if we can afford to make these changes," Yakim said. "But to me, every palace is the same. I just want to be with you. We could be together in Berith's guest suite, and I'd still be happy. I'm not used to this kind of luxury, Lucifer, and it doesn't matter to me."

That was why Lucifer was so deeply in love with Yakim. He never demanded anything for himself. He just wanted Lucifer to be happy. It felt like a miracle that they'd found each other. Lucifer had never thought he could feel like this, but he did, and for the first time since he'd taken his father's place on the throne, the future felt promising.

"As long as you like this place and you trust me, I think we found our palace," he said.

Yakim's smile was everything. "Of course I trust you. The palace is nice enough, but it doesn't matter to me. The fact that you'll live here does."

Lucifer grinned and raised high on his tiptoes to kiss him. Since he looked human, his lovers were often taller and bigger than him. He'd never had a problem with it, but he'd never really enjoyed it, either.

He loved that Yakim towered over him. He loved that Yakim could pin him to the wall and have his way with him, but even more, he loved that Yakim never hesitated to do so and didn't seem afraid to hurt him. He couldn't even if he tried. He wasn't intimidated, and he knew that if he did anything Lucifer didn't enjoy, Lucifer would be vocal about it. For the first time ever, Lucifer didn't have to worry about hiding who he was from the person he was with, and that kind of freedom meant everything to him. He didn't think Yakim understood, but he didn't have to.

His phone vibrated, and with a sigh, he stepped away from his lover. He grinned when he saw that Bretton was calling and quickly answered.

"Are you back yet?"

"Hello to you, too. Yes, I'm fine, thank you for asking."

If Bretton was sarcastic, it probably meant everything had gone the way he'd expected. It was a relief. "You're welcome. Answer my question."

"Yes, I'm back, and I have news. Berith and I are waiting for you in his office. How long will it take you to be back?"

"I'll open a portal into his portal room." Whatever had happened, Lucifer needed to hear it right away.

"Good."

"Can you tell me if it's bad or good news?"

"It's the news we expected. I don't know if it's good or bad, but it is what it is."

That was confirmation that Lucifer's family was involved. Like Bretton had said, it was what he'd expected.

But with confirmation, he could finally do what needed to be done. Then he'd dedicate the rest of his life to making Yakim happy.

Yakim was nervous about what Lucifer would find out about his family, but Lucifer didn't seem to be. He walked down the hallways with intention, almost as if he expected his father and sister to be in the office when he arrived. There was no hesitation in him. He was ready for this to be over, no matter what happened next.

Yakim felt the same, but now that he had his father, he couldn't help but wonder how Lucifer felt about his family being involved. It had to hurt, right? Even though Yakim wasn't close to his mother, he couldn't imagine her actively working against him. It couldn't be easy to deal with something like that, yet Lucifer seemed perfectly all right with it.

Maybe he was used to it. They hadn't talked much about Lucifer's family, something they'd need to rectify, but from the little Yakim knew, this wasn't the first time they'd tried to get the throne. Lucifer's father had been king of Hell before Lucifer, and he hadn't done a great job. No one wanted him to take the throne back, and from what Yakim had heard from gossip around the palace, Lucifer's sister was very much like their father. She wouldn't make a good queen.

But that wouldn't stop her from trying to be one.

Lucifer didn't pause when they reached Berith's office. Sabin didn't try to stop them, either. He looked up when he heard them, then waved them inside.

Yakim was surprised when Lucifer slowed down and then paused. He was waiting for Yakim to walk in first. They'd discussed it, but it wasn't easy for Lucifer to give in. Yakim wanted to be the first to walk into a room to be sure no one there would attack Lucifer. While Lucifer had tried brushing him off before, it seemed to finally get through to him that Yakim would feel better if he allowed him to do it. He didn't doubt that Lucifer could defend himself, and he didn't actually think someone was waiting in Berith's office to hurt him. It was ingrained in him to behave like this because of how long he'd been a bodyguard, and that was that.

Yakim knocked, then opened the door. He stepped in, not one bit surprised to see that Berith and Bretton had company. Lon was here, along with Mel. Yakim gave a quick look around, then nodded. Lucifer came in, closing the door and turning to face the others. His gaze stopped on Bretton, who was on one of the chairs, holding his tablet.

"Tell me," he ordered.

Bretton's expression was serious as he nodded. "As we suspected, your father and your sister are involved."

"Wait," Mel said. "You have a father?" Everyone's attention turned to him. His cheeks flushed, and he looked hesitant, but when no one said anything, he explained, "It's just that everyone always says that you're a fallen angel. I didn't really think about it until now, but I guess that's not the case?"

Lucifer chuckled and shook his head. He went to sit in one of the empty chairs in front of Berith's desk, and since they were all taken now, Yakim stood behind him. He didn't mind. He was used to standing behind the people he protected.

"No, I'm not a fallen angel, although I've heard those stories and find them funny," Lucifer explained. "I was never an angel. I was born a demon, and I have parents."

"And a sister," Bretton grumbled.

"Yes. My father was king of Hell before me, but he never did a great job. That's where we got the reputation of Hell being a place of pain and cruelty. The only thing he ever wanted was power and wealth, and he never hesitated to torture and kill people to obtain that. That was how he behaved, and the other demons in Hell just went along with it and behaved the same way. They knew they wouldn't pay for hurting people or stealing. He quickly realized I disagreed with how he did things, so he decided my sister would eventually take his place on the throne."

"That's obviously not what happened."

"It's not. He believed I was too young to try anything, but I've always been powerful. I knew I was stronger than him, so I challenged him as soon as I was sure I could win a fight. He found it hilarious and agreed to fight me in front of everyone because he thought he'd beat me up and show the court how strong he was. Instead, I won. It was so public that there was no way for him to hide what happened, and by the next morning, half of Hell knew his son had beaten him. That was how I got on the throne, and I've been there since then."

"I understand why your father isn't happy now," Mel said. "I'm surprised you didn't have him killed."

"I try not to behave like him, even when it would be the easiest way to do things. I've allowed him and my sister to live at the palace and continue to enjoy their wealth. It's clear that was a mistake."

Lucifer turned to Bretton, who nodded at him and looked down at his tablet.

"Your father has been funneling money from the palace accounts into his and has been funding the society. I found many payments, including one to your bodyguard. Your father tried to have you killed, and I have proof of it."

"What about Jessamyn?"

"I'm still looking into her, but I have no doubt she's involved, too. There are rumors of a woman working against you, and it can only be her."

Lucifer nodded. Yakim wanted to reach for him, even though he wasn't sure Lucifer was sad about what he'd just learned. He'd expected it, and it was clear he'd had enough of dealing with his family.

Yakim realized that he *could* support Lucifer. In this situation, it was even expected of him. Everyone around them would wonder why he wasn't if he didn't do anything. He was so used to controlling his feelings, especially when it came to Lucifer. Knowing that no one would care if he touched him was odd.

So he did. He reached out and squeezed Lucifer's shoulder. He knew he'd done the right thing when Lucifer looked up at him and smiled before squeezing his hand. He twined their fingers together and held on, and Yakim was happy to give him all the support he needed.

"So, how are you going to deal with them?" Berith asked.

Lucifer sighed. "My first instinct is to confront them."

"That would be the worst thing to do," Bretton said. "They have their allies, just like you have yours."

"I'm going to have to confront them eventually, and you just said you had proof that my father paid my bodyguard to kill me."

"I do. I want more, though. I want proof they're involved with the society, and I'm still looking over those payments."

"How difficult can it be?"

Bretton stared at Lucifer with an arched brow. For a second, everyone was silent.

Lucifer huffed. "I wasn't trying to imply that you don't know how to do your job or that you can't do it. I just want this to be over."

"It will be eventually. We need to find out who's in the society and extirpate them from the court. If you go after your family now, you'll only get the head. It's not enough. The monster would still be there, and if you truly want to start over in a new palace, you have to be sure the entire society is gone."

For a moment, Yakim wondered if Lucifer would throw a tantrum. It wouldn't be like him, but it would be understandable considering what was happening. Not only was the situation with the society frustrating, but he'd just found out his family was involved. He might have expected it, but it still couldn't be easy.

"What do you suggest?" he asked instead.

"Give me a bit more time."

"I want to, but we need to go back. I must show the court I'm fine and still in control."

Bretton nodded. "I've already given orders to ready everything for your return. They know you're coming."

Yakim frowned. "Won't that give Lucifer's family an opportunity to strike? Right now, they can't do much because they don't have any members of the society here anymore, but once he's back, they'll be able to get to him."

"That's what I'm counting on," Lucifer said. "I can punish them much faster. I might also have witnesses, which will help."

Yakim didn't like the sound of that, but he didn't think they had a choice.

CHAPTER SEVENTEEN

Yakim's life was changing too quickly, and he didn't know how to deal with it. When he'd left the palace, he'd been Lucifer's bodyguard. Everyone at the palace had known him as one of Berith's guards, and they'd treated them as such. Now, everything had changed, and Yakim didn't know how to deal with it.

The servants who had treated him like he was one of them before now bowed to him. They kept asking him if he needed anything. A few even seemed afraid of him. He hated that, but he didn't know how to change it. He wasn't sure he could.

He wasn't just a bodyguard anymore. He was Lucifer's consort, and that was how everyone was treating him. It didn't change who he was as a person, but clearly, many people thought it did. Either that, or they believed Yakim would punish them for not treating him with deference.

Nothing could be further from the truth.

He didn't know how to behave, which was why he just nodded at the servant bowing at him and walked past her.

Roque, who was walking next to him, snickered. "I thought she was going to faint," he said.

"It's not funny. They all treat me differently, and I don't like it."

"What did you expect? You shacked up with the king of Hell. I should bow to you, too."

Yakim stopped walking. "Don't you dare."

"I'd never do it. I know you too well, so I'm aware of the fact that you don't want anyone to bow to you. I don't because

I'm your friend, but you have to understand where everyone else is coming from. They don't want to be punished, and even though they knew you as a bodyguard, they know you're not just that anymore. It's their job to follow the hierarchy, and right now, you're the second most powerful demon in Hell."

The thought made Yakim want to scream. He wasn't powerful. He was good at his job and proud of that, but what could he do with so much power? He didn't think he could guide Hell even if he tried. He definitely wasn't going to attempt it. The throne was safe in Lucifer's hands, and Yakim wanted nothing to do with it.

He'd always known his life would change if he agreed to date Lucifer. He'd even known how it would change and that people would see him differently.

That didn't mean he had to like it.

At least he still had his friends and his father. Frank had been impressed by the fact that Yakim was dating the king of Hell, but it hadn't changed anything between them. Yakim was still his son, and that was how he treated him. Roque had never bowed to Yakim, and he wouldn't start now. As for Mel and Berith and their other close friends, Yakim had warned them that he'd leave the room if they even tried it. For some reason, Mel had found that hilarious, but Berith had assured Yakim that no matter what he was now, he was still their friend.

That was all Yakim wanted. He didn't care about the throne, power, or anything related. The only thing he cared about was the people he considered family, and as long as they treated him like they always had, he thought he could get used to this.

That belief was shattered when he and Roque reached Berith's office. Berith had asked to see Yakim, so Roque waved at him and left, probably to go find Mel. He'd spent the morning in the suite he shared with Berith, so he'd been safe.

Now that Yakim was alone, he felt more hesitant, but there was no way around this.

He'd known Berith would have to part ways with him once it was clear that he and Lucifer were serious about each other. It hadn't happened so far, but Yakim was pretty sure that was why Berith had asked him to see him today.

It wasn't, or at least not entirely.

When he walked into the office after Sabin waved him in, it was to find that Berith wasn't alone. Bretton was with him, and he got to his feet instantly and bowed.

Yakim resisted the urge to roll his eyes. "You wanted to see me?" he asked, turning his attention to Berith.

"I did, actually," Bretton said.

He was a little stiff, and Yakim wondered if he was like that because he knew he wouldn't like whatever Bretton said.

"What do you need from me?"

"As the king's consort, you need a bodyguard," Bretton said, going straight to the point.

Yakim appreciated that. He *didn't* appreciate the suggestion that he couldn't defend himself. "I don't."

"You do. I realize you've been a bodyguard for a long time and that you can defend yourself. That's a good thing, because it means you won't have to just rely on your bodyguards to protect you. It doesn't change the fact that now that you're with Lucifer, people are going to try to get to you. You can't always have eyes everywhere, which means you need someone to protect you."

Yakim looked at Berith for help, but the prince shook his head.

"He's right," Berith said. "You're not just Yakim anymore. You have to deal with the consequences of that, unfortunately."

It was clear that nothing Yakim would say would change

their minds. Logically, he knew they were right. If it had been anyone but him in his place, he would have insisted they have one bodyguard at the very least. He might not like it, but there was no way out of it.

"Who?"

"I'm still trying to decide," Bretton said, raising his head. "I asked Berith to give me a list of people he and Lon trust with their lives. I'm looking into the background of all of them."

He wanted to be sure that what happened with Lucifer's bodyguard didn't happen again. It was understandable and hopefully meant that Yakim had a few more days of freedom. "I understand. What do you need from me?"

"I'd like for you to go over the list. You've worked with these people, and it would be best if you trusted your body-guard. I also wanted to ask you to go along with this, and I'm glad you're not fighting it as hard as I expected you to."

"Fighting it won't help me, will it? I expected my life to change when I started dating Lucifer, and I knew this was coming. I might not like it, but I don't want to make anyone's life harder." He sighed. "Give me that list. I'll go over it and tell you who I think would be best suited for the role." Yakim might not be able to avoid having a bodyguard, but if he could choose who he wanted to watch his back, maybe things wouldn't be that bad.

Not everything in Lucifer's life was a disaster. He'd begrudg-ingly agreed to let Bretton dig deeper into his father and sis-ter's lives, which meant he couldn't return to his old palace, kick their asses, and finally focus on his future with Yakim. He had to *wait*, something he didn't enjoy.

Thankfully, he had plenty of things to distract him. Mainly, he was spending a lot of time with Yakim, and since they'd

finally decided which palace they wanted, it was only the be-
ginning.

The palace was much smaller than the one Lucifer had in-
herited from his father, and he liked it that way. Yakim had
seemed to like the bathtub in the main suite especially, and
they'd agreed to tear down the walls that separated the two
smaller suites and make a big one for both of them. Berith had
graciously offered some of his people for the work, and Lucifer was excited to see what would come out of it. He hadn't
seen the place yet between the renovations and the cleaning,
and he was excited.

But there was still a dark cloud on the horizon. How could
he enjoy his future when he knew his father and his sister
would continue coming after him unless he put a stop to it?
He was tempted to sneak back to the old palace and ignore
Bretton's order to stay away from them, but Bretton would
kick his ass if he tried it, and Lucifer didn't want that.

He was still thinking about it when he walked into his
suite. It was odd not to have Yakim with him, but Berith had
asked to see him, and Lucifer had reassured him that he could
be without protection for a half-hour. He hadn't done much,
anyway. He'd taken a walk through the garden on his way
back to his suite, and now, he was ready to work.

He didn't get the opportunity to do so because he found
Yakim sitting on the couch when he walked in. He was staring
at his hands in his lap, and for a second, Lucifer thought
something was wrong. He'd never been afraid of being left by
any of his lovers, but he couldn't imagine a life without Yakim
anymore.

"Did something happen?" he asked as he rushed to his
lover's side.

Yakim blinked up at him. He smiled, and Lucifer relaxed,
but he still didn't know what was wrong.

"Nothing happened. Bretton wanted to see me about my

new bodyguard."

That would do it. Yakim was used to *being* the bodyguard, so it made sense that he didn't enjoy the thought of having one. It was one more step into his new relationship with Lucifer and becoming the king's consort. Every time something changed like that, Lucifer expected him to have enough and decide he wasn't worth it. So far, Yakim was here, but maybe this would be the straw that broke the camel's back.

"Did you tell him to fuck off?" Lucifer asked as he sat on the couch next to Yakim.

"I was tempted, but he and Berith are right. I'm your consort, and as such, I need more protection than I can provide myself. At least they're giving me the choice of who I want to follow me around every day."

He didn't sound angry but rather annoyed. That was enough to tell Lucifer that he didn't regret being with him. He might not like needing a bodyguard, but he wouldn't argue.

Lucifer bumped their shoulders together. "Now you know how I feel. I don't need a bodyguard, but I always have someone following me around. It makes Bretton happy."

"It makes me happy, too. But if I need a bodyguard, you need one, too. Or is this going to be a bodyguard who has a bodyguard situation? Because I don't think that's going to work."

And now Lucifer was in Yakim's place and understood precisely why he was annoyed. "Fine. I'll talk to Bretton and choose someone."

Yakim grinned. "You're not going to argue that you don't need protection?"

"I'm not because I know that you'll do the same, and I want you to be as protected as possible."

He leaned against Yakim, happy when Yakim wrapped an arm around his shoulders. They were still finding their way into this relationship, but things were especially hard for

Yakim. His entire life had changed because he'd fallen in love with Lucifer, and Lucifer couldn't do anything about it. The only way to stop would be to leave Yakim, but Lucifer was selfish and would never do something like that. Unless Yakim asked, he was in this for the long term.

He opened his mouth to tell Yakim that he loved him when the door slammed open, making both of them jump. Yakim reacted like the bodyguard he was. He got to his feet and placed himself between Lucifer and the door, ready to defend him if whoever had arrived was a threat.

Lucifer got up, too, and glanced around his lover. Yes, the new arrival was a threat, and he was tempted to tell Yakim to kill her.

Instead, he pressed a hand against Yakim's back and stepped around him. Yakim's entire body was tense, and he wouldn't be happy if Lucifer strayed too far from him, so Lucifer stayed next to him and faced his sister. "Jessamyn," he drawled. "To what do I owe this pleasure?"

"You're moving?" she asked.

Her tone wasn't nice. Clearly, she didn't like the thought of Lucifer moving, but Lucifer couldn't say why. He didn't care, either. "I see you've heard of my new palace. Is that why you're here?"

"Of course it's why I'm here. You can't move. The king's palace has always been the same and always will be."

The sound of people running in the hallway made Lucifer glance behind her. He wasn't surprised to see two guards there, but they appeared hesitant, possibly because of who Jessamyn was. They didn't want to get in trouble with Lucifer by dragging his sister out of the suite like they should. As far as Lucifer knew, she hadn't been invited by Berith, and she had no authority to barge in the way she had.

"What's going on here?" Berith's voice boomed as he walked in.

Lucifer kept his body relaxed. He didn't want his sister to know how angry he was and that she was getting at him. "My sister decided to visit, apparently. I take it she didn't reach out to you first?"

"Neither she nor your father did, yet they're both here." Berith gestured, and Lon and his second in command dragged Lucifer's father in.

Lucifer eyed him. He didn't feel love or even affection for Genon. If he felt anything at all, it was annoyance and a bit of hatred. He wasn't surprised that his father was causing trouble, especially since his sister was involved, too, but he wished he didn't have to deal with them.

How had Bretton not found out they were coming? It wasn't like him, but maybe he'd been so focused on what they were up to that he hadn't seen the signs, or maybe Jessamyn and Genon hadn't planned this. Lucifer wouldn't be surprised if his sister had just found out about the new palace and acted without thinking, and his father had gone along to try to stop her.

Lucifer's father tried to shake off the hands keeping him in place, but thankfully, they didn't let go.

"How dare you touch me?" he bellowed. "I am your king."

Lucifer chuckled. "I'm afraid you're living in the past. You haven't been king in decades." He looked at Lon. "Keep him there, please."

"Of course, your Highness," Lon said, slightly bowing his head.

Lucifer stared at his sister and father. He'd wanted to confront them, but Bretton had forbidden him to do so. They'd come to him, so technically, Lucifer hadn't broken his promise to his personal assistant. He could get rid of them without doing so, and the thought made him smile.

Yakim didn't know what to do. He was behaving as Lucifer's bodyguard, and he couldn't think of anything but pulling Lucifer behind his back and protecting him, but at the same time, he was Lucifer's consort. He should stand beside Lucifer the way he was now and face Lucifer's family with him. He was being torn in two different directions, and it was infuriating and confusing.

Yakim had to trust Lucifer to know what he was doing and be able to defend himself if his father or his sister attacked him. Instead of pushing him back like he yearned to, he stood tall and stared at them like Lucifer was.

Yakim couldn't remember ever seeing this expression on Lucifer's face. He was staring at his family as if they were nothing more than insects on the ground. It was like he was wondering if he should squash them, and maybe he wanted to, but he couldn't be bothered because they were just that unimportant. It wasn't like him, and it showed Yakim a side of Lucifer he hadn't known.

He didn't like it, but he understood the need for it. If Lucifer didn't show how ruthless he was, people would attack him to take his place, and he couldn't allow that to happen.

Neither could Yakim.

"Now, are you here only because you wished to yell at me about my new palace?" Lucifer asked.

"I'm your sister," Jessamyn snapped. "I should be the first to know about these things."

"You might have been if you behaved like my sister, but you never have. What do you want?"

She stood up straighter. Yakim expected her to be defiant and say that she wanted the throne, but she didn't. She was surrounded by powerful demons. She might be the king's sister, but even Berith was above her in Hell's hierarchy.

"We weren't told about your palace," she repeated.

"That's because we only told the people we want to move

there."

"We're not part of those people?"

"Why would you be? Neither of you will be invited to move with me. You can stay in the old palace for as long as you want. I won't ever be returning to it."

"This isn't the way to be king," Lucifer's father said. "You have brought shame to Hell. I should never have allowed you to take my place on the throne. You're ruining everything."

Lucifer snorted. "Because I don't want Hell to be lawless? I suppose I'm ruining your idea of Hell and the only way you ever had to be important, but I don't care."

Someone by the door gasped, and everyone turned to look at Mel. His eyes were wide as he stared at the situation happening in front of him. He didn't move, but Berith did. He rushed to his side and wrapped an arm around his shoulders to pull him against his side.

"You're allowing this to continue," Jessamyn spat out. "Demons taking humans as consort." Her gaze flickered to Yakim, and he tensed. "And you took a bodyguard as your lover. I thought you'd have more sense than that."

Lucifer's body tensed, and Yakim waited for him to react to his sister's words. He stayed where he was, though. Yakim wondered for a moment if he was going to hide that they were together, but instead, he took Yakim's hand and linked their fingers together. "That's where you're wrong. I didn't take Yakim as my lover. I'm taking him as my consort."

Jessamyn's face turned red. Her skin was pale, and she looked human, like Lucifer. They were both beautiful. She had the same long black hair as her brother, his pale skin, and his black eyes. She wore a long dress that emphasized how slender and elegant she was. There was a quiet strength in Lucifer but not in Jessamyn. It was clear to anyone watching her that she was nothing more than a snake waiting to strike.

"You can't," she argued.

"The last time I checked, I was still king and could do what I wanted. Yakim will be a perfect consort."

Yakim briefly wondered if Jessamyn's head was going to explode. He hoped it would, but he doubted things would be that easy.

Lucifer had just told her that a mere bodyguard was now above her in the hierarchy. Like every other demon in Hell, she'd have to obey Yakim's orders. For someone who was desperately trying to get on the throne, it had to be infuriating.

Yakim loved to see it.

"You're ruining everything," she yelled. "This isn't what Hell should be like. It was perfect, and you ruined it, and I won't allow you to continue doing so."

Yakim tensed as she threw herself at Lucifer. Even though he was Lucifer's consort, part of him still warned him that he needed to be careful handling her. This was the king's sister, not just any demon. At the same time, though, she was attacking Lucifer, and Yakim couldn't allow that to happen. He'd defend his lover, whatever it took. He wouldn't hesitate even if he had to kill Jessamyn.

But she wasn't the only one moving. Lucifer's father had knocked off Lon's hands and turned to Berith, who was pushing Mel behind his back. This was the worst-case scenario, but it looked like Jessamyn and Lucifer's father hadn't thought about where they had decided to attack Lucifer.

They might be vipers, but they were in a mongoose nest.

Lucifer almost rolled his eyes when his sister threw himself at him. Did she really think she was going to win a physical fight with him—or any fight, for that matter? She was strong, but he was stronger, and he was surrounded by allies. Even if Lucifer was unwilling to raise a hand to his sister, plenty of other people wouldn't hesitate.

The first was Yakim. Lucifer understood he could defend himself and was even eager to watch it happen because Yakim was incredibly sexy, but he didn't trust his sister not to hurt his consort. He didn't want anything to happen to Yakim, which meant this had to be over as soon as possible. Besides, Lucifer had enough of dealing with his sister and his father. He'd been happy to ignore them while they plotted behind his back, but now, they'd confronted him, and he had enough.

To no one's surprise, Yakim moved to place himself between Lucifer and Jessamyn. She wouldn't hesitate to hurt him, but Yakim appeared hesitant to touch her. Maybe it was because she was a female, or maybe because she was Lucifer's sister. Whatever the reason, it didn't matter.

Lucifer raised both hands. Time froze, and while he could only keep this up for a few moments, it was all he needed.

With a wave of his hand, only Jessamyn and Genon stayed frozen while everyone else started moving again. Yakim turned his wide eyes to Lucifer, and Lucifer arched a brow when that was all he did. He was so shocked he didn't even move to restrain Jessamyn.

"I can keep this up for a while, but I'd rather not," Lucifer drawled.

Yakim finally moved. He and the guards tied up both Lucifer's sister and his father. It was anticlimactic. They'd come here for a fight, probably expecting to be able to kill Lucifer or, at the very least, injure him. They hadn't even touched him.

But Jessamyn had made the way she felt about him obvious, and Lucifer didn't like it.

He waited until they were both tied up to unfreeze them. It hadn't taken him a lot of energy to keep them frozen, and his anger had fueled his power.

Jessamyn's eyes widened, and she pulled onto the ties keeping her in place, but she couldn't move.

"You'll pay for this!" she screamed.

"Will I? You just tried to attack your king. How did that go for you? Because from where I stand, it would have been better if you'd continued living your life of wealth and pleasure without coming after me. Now, you'll lose all of that. Is that what you wanted, Jessamyn? What was your goal?"

"I was supposed to be the queen."

Lucifer had always known that was one of the main problems between them. Their father had always pushed them against one another and made promises he hadn't kept. He'd told Jessamyn she would be queen, but instead, Lucifer had become king. It wasn't their father's fault, because he'd done everything he could to stop it from happening, but Lucifer had been stronger. If Jessamyn hadn't been so much like their father, Lucifer might have been happy with her on the throne, but he couldn't risk it. She'd ruin everything he'd worked so hard to obtain over the past decades.

Lucifer was nothing like their father, but she was exactly like him, and he'd almost brought Hell to ruins. He'd turned it into a landscape of pain and blood, and Lucifer would make sure that would never happen again.

He looked at the guards. "Take them away."

Two of them moved forward to grab Jessamyn, but she screamed and launched herself at them. The ties around her wrists snapped, and there was a flash of silver when she raised her arms. She pushed one of the guards away while slamming her hand against the chest of the other guard. He screamed and fell to his knees, and she took the opportunity to dart toward the door while Lucifer grabbed the guard on his way down.

Genon and the guard holding his arm were in the way. Genon moved toward Jessamyn, maybe because he hoped she'd take him with her as she escaped. Instead, she pushed him to the side so hard that he stumbled and fell. He cried out and called for her, but she didn't even slow down. She was out the door before anyone could stop her.

"Find her," Berith snapped.

The guards moved to obey. They disappeared down the hallway, and the room was silent for a moment. Lucifer lowered the guard to the floor and took a step back. He looked around and wondered if he wanted to continue staying here. His new palace wasn't in great shape yet, but he'd be willing to sleep on the floor if it meant he wouldn't have to spend one more second in this room.

Lucifer didn't care about Genon and Jessamyn, but knowing that his own blood had plotted against him still annoyed him. He'd expected it and wasn't surprised, but he wasn't happy. He supposed he and Yakim were lucky that they had at least one parent who cared between the two of them. Frank had been nothing but nice and sweet with Yakim, which was what he needed. Lucifer supposed that as long as Yakim was happy, he didn't need any more family.

"What did she do to the guard?" Mel asked.

Lucifer looked at him to find that he'd left Berith's side and was kneeling next to the guard his sister had hit. Lucifer went to join him. When he pressed a hand against the guard's chest, he felt blood seeping from a wound.

"You should call the healer," he told Mel as he quickly cut open the guard's shirt with one of the guard's daggers.

There was a deep but small wound in the middle of his chest, as if Jessamyn had used something long but sharp and thin. Blood bubbled out, a sure sign that she'd hit a lung.

"I'll take care of him," Lon said as he knelt next to Lucifer.

"I'm sorry this happened."

"Not your fault."

But Lucifer couldn't help but feel guilty. Without his sister, the guard wouldn't be wounded.

He got to his feet and hovered there, wishing he could do more. For all of his power, he couldn't heal demons, and it made him feel like he wasn't enough. What good was being the king of Hell when he couldn't even do this?

A hand on his shoulder startled him. He turned to find Yakim standing next to him. Once he had Lucifer's attention, Yakim guided him toward Berith and Mel.

"This wasn't your fault," he murmured. "Your sister and your father are at fault, but you're not. She's the one who wounded the guard."

Yakim was right, but even if he wasn't, Lucifer couldn't afford to let these feelings take him down. His father was still in the room, ranting while two guards held him by the arms. Lucifer didn't need to listen to know what he was saying. He and Jessamyn had always had the same goals, and that hadn't changed.

They wanted the throne. They'd made a play for it, and they'd lost.

Lucifer glanced at the door. There were no signs of the guards or of Jessamyn, and unease gripped him. His father would soon be behind bars, but what about his sister? She was the more dangerous of the two, especially after she'd calmed down and thought about what she was doing. If the guards didn't catch her, Lucifer would have to look over his shoulder until he was sure she was dealt with. He didn't like the thought of that, especially since he'd been planning on living a happy life with Yakim.

But it felt good to know that whatever happened with his sister, he wouldn't face all of this alone. Yakim would be standing right next to him, giving him strength, support, and, more importantly, love. Together, they would change Hell.

EPILOGUE

The guard bowed at Yakim as he opened the door to let him in. Yakim was tempted to ask him not to do so, but he'd already tried, and the results hadn't been great. Either the guards and servants were offended because they thought Yakim believed they weren't good enough to serve him, or they were terrified because they expected him to try to get them to make a mistake. It was infuriating that they could believe something like that of him, but Lucifer had gently reminded him that they'd had to deal with Jessamyn and Genon for decades, and those two had been cruel enough to play that kind of game.

Yakim hated it. He could even say he hated them, even though he barely knew them. He had no intention of ever trying to get to know Lucifer's father, and as for Jessamyn, she was in the wind.

She'd managed to sneak out of the palace, leaving behind more wounded guards and a dead servant in her wake. Everyone was looking for her, but Yakim suspected no one would find her. She was smart and sneaky, and she had a goal. She wanted the throne and was ready to do anything to obtain it. She hadn't hesitated to kill to save herself, and she'd abandoned her father. She was ruthless, and even though Bretton had frozen all of her accounts and taken away everything he could, everyone knew this wasn't over. She'd probably funneled more money into other accounts and in hiding places, which meant she'd be back.

It hadn't been the best way to start a life together, but

Yakim and Lucifer had done their best to ignore all of that. Their new palace had been renovated, and they'd moved in a few days ago.

That was when things *really* changed. When they'd been at Berith's palace, the servants had known Yakim as a bodyguard. Even after he and Lucifer had gotten together, they'd still treated him like one rather than like the king's consort. Yakim had liked that and wished it could have continued, but it hadn't. The servants at the new palace were the servants Lucifer had used before moving there, and as soon as they'd found out that Yakim was Lucifer's consort, they'd started treating him accordingly. They bowed to him, asked him if there was anything they could do for him, and waited for his orders. They treated him with a reverence he wasn't used to, and it would take him a while to wrap his mind around it.

But even though his mind was a mess and Jessamyn was in the wind, there were many positives. Yakim grinned as he walked into Lucifer's office and saw that he was hard at work with Bretton. They both looked up when they heard him, and while Bretton glared, Lucifer got up immediately and walked around his desk. He opened his arms, and Yakim stepped between them. He wrapped his arms around Lucifer's shoulders and kissed the top of his head, and for a moment, he was at peace.

"I didn't expect you to visit me in my office," Lucifer said.

"I didn't say anything because I knew Bretton wouldn't be happy."

"You're right. I'm not," Bretton said.

Yakim grinned at him. They were still getting to know each other, but he liked Bretton. Bretton had Lucifer's best interests at heart, and he was one of Lucifer's best friends. He and Yakim wanted the same thing.

To keep Lucifer safe and happy.

"Well, I'm sorry to bother you, but I know what Lucifer's

been planning, and he's not going without me."

Lucifer stepped away. He didn't look at Yakim, which was a sure sign he was still trying to hide his plan.

Bretton snickered. "So he's in trouble? I'm not angry at you anymore. I really want to see this."

"Why don't you go back to your office?" Lucifer said. "Yakim and I have something to do."

"Now it's Yakim and you? He just said you didn't tell him you were going to visit your father."

Lucifer hadn't. No matter how many times Yakim told him he didn't need to be shielded from this kind of thing, it was as if Lucifer was convinced he'd break down if he found out about threats against his life. Maybe it was because things had just become official between them. Lucifer had to understand that Yakim would never be a normal consort. He couldn't be like Mel and allow people around him to protect him. He might have been forced to accept a bodyguard, but that didn't mean he wouldn't do everything he could to protect Lucifer.

"I didn't want him to worry," Lucifer muttered.

Yakim cupped the back of his head with one hand. "I already told you not to do this. I want to know what's going on."

"It's not your job to keep me safe anymore."

"It might not be my job, but it doesn't mean I'm going to stop. Besides, this isn't about protecting you. It's about supporting you while you face your father for the first time since he and your sister attacked you."

Things hadn't gone like they'd expected. Yakim had thought they'd have more of a fight on their hands, but Lucifer's power had stopped them before they could do any damage. Yakim knew he still felt guilty about not stopping his sister when she got away, but even though Lucifer was powerful, he was still only one demon. No one would expect him to fight this on his own.

He certainly didn't.

They were silent as they left the office and headed toward the jail cells under the palace. Lucifer hadn't left his father with Berith. He'd wanted to have him close so that they could interrogate him, but so far, he had given the interrogators any of the answers they needed. He'd refused to talk about Jessamyn, the society, and their plan to take the throne.

He wasn't sure it mattered. The only answer they really needed at the moment was where Jessamyn was, but the rest was inconsequential. The society was gone without its leaders at the head. Bretton was still digging to find out every member because he wanted to know who had worked against Lucifer, but Yakim doubted any of them would try anything against the king. Jessamyn was the only one who might, which was why they needed to find her. She wasn't making it easy for them, but Yakim was convinced that, eventually, they'd get her. Either that or she'd attack again, and this time, Yakim would make sure she didn't run.

"I know I should have told you about this," Lucifer said.

"You should have. I understand why you didn't, though, so it's fine."

Lucifer stopped in front of the door that would lead them downstairs. "I shouldn't try so hard to protect you. It's just hard for me to remember when I panic at the thought of anything happening to you."

Yakim pulled Lucifer into his arms. "Don't you think I feel the same? I might know that you're all-powerful, but you're still the man I love. Thinking about anything happening to you, especially when it comes to your father and your sister, makes me panic. That's why I don't want you to do this alone. I know you can defend yourself from your father and that he's behind bars, but I feel like if I'm not with you when you see him, something bad will happen to you."

Lucifer chuckled and reached up to kiss Yakim. "I guess

both of us need to learn not to be overprotective."

"I'm not sure how that's going to work, but I'm willing to try as long as you are."

Lucifer nodded. "We'll work on it together."

That was the only right answer.

Yakim hadn't expected Lucifer's father to give them anything new, so he wasn't surprised when they left an hour later without any answers. He didn't think Lucifer was, either.

"I don't think he actually knows where your sister is," Yakim said.

Lucifer nodded. "He expects her to be loyal to him, but he doesn't understand her. She's not loyal to anyone but herself. She used him as an ally because he was there and made things easier for her, but she's not going to worry about him now that he's locked up. She's certainly not going to come for him."

Lucifer was still in danger, but they'd gone from having the entire society against him to just one person. Lucifer would make sure Jessamyn couldn't touch Lucifer.

And if she tried, he'd stop her.

Lucifer had never been so happy, even though he'd just left the jail. It was an odd activity to do with the man he loved, but he should have known that Yakim wouldn't let him talk to his father on his own. He also should have known that his father wouldn't tell him anything about Jessamyn, and he had, but he'd still hoped.

He was happy, but he'd worry until he was sure Jessamyn was under control. It didn't matter that Yakim could defend himself. Jessamyn was dangerous, and she was coming for them and the throne. If they weren't careful, she might hurt one of them or their friends, and that wasn't something Lucifer was willing to consider.

But for now, there was nothing he could do. Jessamyn was in hiding. The rest of the society had disbanded and was doing the same, but Bretton was working on finding out every member and getting rid of them. It would take time, but Lucifer was sure he'd do it, and Lucifer and Yakim would be safer.

But not completely safe until Jessamyn was found.

Lucifer wished he didn't have to worry about his sister, but maybe he didn't have to. Worrying wouldn't help. He needed to continue living as if she weren't a danger. Otherwise, he'd let her win, and that wasn't something he was willing to do.

"Do you have anything planned for the rest of the day?" Yakim asked as they walked down the hallway.

"I can play hooky."

Yakim laughed. "Where did you hear that expression?"

"Mel."

They'd been talking almost every day on the phone and through emails. Lucifer hadn't expected to get so close to Berith's consort, but it was impossible not to love Mel. He was a sweetheart who made Berith happy, and Lucifer would always have a soft spot for him.

They were like a big family, something Lucifer never had while growing up. It was another thing that brought him happiness, and he couldn't believe how much his life had changed with just a visit to Berith. Lucifer couldn't imagine not having him, Mel, and the others.

No matter what Jessamyn was plotting, she wouldn't take this away from him. Lucifer's life was full of joy now, and he'd do whatever he could not to lose the blissful peace his family gave him. He had a duty to Hell and its inhabitants, but his loyalty and love went to his family.

About the Author

Catherine is the creator of several series, most of them paranormal, including the Whitedell Pride Series and the Gillham Pack Series. While she graduated in translation, she decided to go the writer's way because it was more fun to create her own stories and characters.

She's been living in Italy for more than twenty years, but she's a daughter of the North—Belgium to be precise—and she misses it so much that she's already planning to move back.

She loves pizza—probably too much—her son, her pets, and of course, books. She sneaks some reading time into her schedule every time she has five minutes free from writing, demands from her various pets and son, and lastly, housework.

Connect with her:

lievens.catherine@gmail.com
BookBub: https://www.bookbub.com/authors/catherine-lievens
Website: https://authorcatherinelievens.com/
Facebook: https://www.facebook.com/catherine.lievens.9
Facebook Group: https://www.facebook.com/groups/411788002341528/
Twitter: https://twitter.com/authorCLievens
Newsletter: http://eepurl.com/c-uvKn

www.ingramcontent.com/pod-product-compliance
Lightning Source LLC
Chambersburg PA
CBHW070850120626
46556CB00002B/939